THE LAST LAP

RETIREMENT HOME FOR RACING WHIPPETS & "TRUBULSOM PORQUAPINES"

A SATIRE

A K MCBALLS

INDELIBLE INK PRESS

Published in 2025 by Indelible Ink Press, Australia

ISBN: 978-0-9942310-1-7

Editorial & Design: Karin Cox, editorandauthor.com

Illustrations by Marlon at GetYourBookIllustrations

Design features: CanvaPro

ACKNOWLEDGMENTS

This book was written almost exclusively in airport lounges and while flying and drinking wine. Ace would like to thank all the kind staff at Qantas for being so nice to him, and the pilots for not crashing.

This book would not have been possible without the creative inspiration provided by the talented winemakers of the Barossa Valley. Ace's editor, Karin, put lots of work into the book, for which she will receive very little reward.

CHAPTER 1

THE WHITE SWAN

Winklebutty was a small, scenic village somewhere near nowhere anybody in their right mind would care to visit. For a short period, the discovery of a rare species of black truffle in its mountain regions had sparked the so-called Fungus Rush of Eighty-eight. Thousands of prospectors and their pigs had hastened to the town, hoping to make their fortune, and, for a while, they did. When the truffle was later discovered to have caused a near-lethal malignant toe fungus (MTF), the rush halted as quickly as it had started.

Now, when people visited Winklebutty, it was either because they had gotten lost on their way to Lumpy Bottom or because they'd been exiled with a fungal infection: Winklebutty also being home to the Holy Spirit Hospital for Tinea, Fungus and Toe Jam Infections, the only such hospital in all the Upper Colon Counties.

Following the discovery of MTF, a concerted military weedicide campaign resulted in a significant reduction in black truffles. Unfortunately, that did nothing to reduce the skyrocketing rates of MTF.

In time, doctors discovered that MTF had nothing at all to

do with black truffles. It was instead caused by poor foot hygiene attributed to a local tradition that discouraged the washing of sports socks during the summer months. By this time, however, the aerial spraying campaign had created an ecological disaster so great that it would take government officials and scientists decades to create a bigger one.

If, for whatever reason, you did end up in Winklebutty, and you walked from the hospital to the end of Tinkle Lane, past the old brewery, way past the sugar mill, down an old road, over a small mountain and down a steep gully, you'd find an old timber building. In its better days, it had been a fashionable health retreat for snooty, wealthy types. In more recent years, however, the White Swan had fallen upon hard times.

The original owner, Sir Martin Frapper, had made some ill-advised financial investments, risking a sizeable portion of his wealth on the whale wee perfume industry. What remained, he lost gambling. Financially destitute, he had sold the White Swan to a German viceroy, who sold it to an Indian raja, who gifted it to his son, who lost it on a bet with the current owner: Angeli Cup.

Neither noble nor wealthy, Angeli was a small woman with a sufficiently bad temper and a tendency to use it not at all sparingly. In her younger days, she had been a stunt pilot, circus clown, businessperson and, finally, a successful jockey. She did not miss the excitement all the time.

At the end of her racing career, Angeli had retired to Winklebutty, which, having never fully recovered from the Fungus Crash, had become a ghost town. Angeli liked the anonymity Winklebutty provided. The White Swan was well hidden between Peppermint Peak and Mount Mountain, far away from the piercing eyes of the racing fraternity paparazzi, and it was one of the few places untouched by the aerial fungus spraying. Wild mushrooms still proliferated there, and as a lifelong vegetarian and lover of mushrooms – one of the few viable non-meat alternatives available – it seemed the perfect place for Angeli and her whippets to retire.

Angeli was tired of the pressures of the racing life and of the constant hounding (literally!) by the press. She longed for a quiet life and dreamt of retiring to her own farm, far from the limelight, the reporters, and from marsupials. She loved all animals except, through an ironic twist of fate, wombats, to which she was extremely allergic.

Angeli had won the White Swan from Raj Pompadour Junior in a vigorous and somewhat heated game of Scrabble®, the outcome of which is mired in controversy to this day. The Raj still refuses to believe that 'bumfat' is a real word in the English language. Nonetheless, he accepted the ruling of the official Scrabble adjudicator, Mr Schiessenburger, and dutifully signed the White Swan over to Angeli.

Angeli had left the Swan almost completely unchanged, except for the sign hanging above the front door. She had removed the old sign, which read 'Ye Old Swan', and hammered in an old wooden plank in its place. Carved on the wood in faded lettering was the following:

CHAPTER 2

A MISCHIEVOUS PORCUPINE, EVEN BY PORCUPINE STANDARDS

"Don't even think about it!" Sally-Dee Pickles spoke in a firm but cheerful tone. She did not have to look at Rex for him to know she was talking to him. Rex raised two of his side quills, which, for porcupines, is the universally accepted way to feign innocence.

It did not work on Sally. For one thing, she wasn't a porcupine, so the significance of the quills completely eluded her. For another, she knew him all too well, and he was never, ever, anytime, innocent of anything whatsoever – ever!

Rex was a mischievous porcupine, even by porcupine standards. His favourite trick was to pretend to be a pillow by curling up and retracting his spines. Most of the whippets at the farm were aware of his shenanigans and were immediately suspicious of a soft, inviting brown pillow appearing unexpectedly in their beds. Destiny, however, was unable to detect the not-at-all-subtle difference between a pillow and an up-to-no-good porcupine.

Rex would sneak into Destiny's bed and transform. Destiny would leap onto her bed only to be greeted by Rex's now-erect spines. For Rex's part, he had insisted for months now that he'd been sleepwalking. Sally-Dee, however, was not to be fooled. She caught him out regularly.

"Get back to your own bed!" she growled playfully, as Rex began to make snoring sounds. "And don't give me that sleepwalking codswallop. Back to your bed, right now, or you'll get toilet brush duties for the week."

Rex made a gargling noise with his nostrils, which is the teenage porcupine equivalent of saying, "Whatever, Mum," in a dismissive tone. The gesture would, unfortunately, be wasted on Sally, who did not know porcupine social cues. Destiny just chuckled to herself in a doggy sort of whippet-type laugh.

Whippet laughter is difficult to describe, or even imitate, but it can be likened to the sound of a pillow being mistreated. Destiny had, in fact, learnt early on to tell the somewhat obvious difference between a soft brown satin pillow appearing suddenly out of nowhere, and Rex's rotund, spiky body. But she had grown fond of his jokes and was often happy to play along. Years of whippet racing had also made her hindquarters very tough and impervious to porcupine bristles, so sitting on Rex felt much like sitting on a vibrating massage chair. Besides, over the years, Destiny had found her own way of playing practical jokes on Rex. Mostly, the jokes resulted in Rex ending up in a nearby creek or toilet bowl. Rex did not find these jokes anywhere near as amusing as Destiny did.

Sally-Dee Pickles had only just started working at the Last Lap, but she was a fast learner. She was born in the Duchy of Frankenfart to an unemployed shoe salesperson father and a casual street juggler mother. (Now that I think of it, it may have been the other way around. For all intents and purposes, it does not matter to the story's progression, so let's just assume her dad was the salesperson – or don't. I really don't care.)

As a child, Sally was short, pimply and very shy. As an adult, she was slightly taller. Over her nose usually sat a pair of purple-rimmed reading glasses. What they were doing there was not always clear, since Sally did not read. Without them, however, she had tendency to bump into doors.

As a teenager, she had suffered the tragic loss of both her parents in a freak water-skiing accident. She never fully recovered from this tragedy. To this day, she blames herself for their death, for it was she who had filled the family boat with the incorrect fuel. In truth, she was not at all at fault for the accident, which had been caused by her father being distracted by a school of tuna and driving directly into a cruise liner. Had he not made this fatal error, he and his wife would have lived another ten minutes before the incorrect fuel mixture caused their boat to explode. If they had survived the initial blast, they would have likely been eaten by the shiver of sharks chasing the tuna.

Sally-Dee, of course, could not have known this. She would spend the next few years in the Frankenfart Orphanage for Children Without Parents, or FOCWOP as it had been affectionately named by people who did not like children.

When she was old enough, she packed her suitcase and left for the Lower Colon Counties, desperate to leave her past behind her. Her past, however, felt lonely without her so decided to follow Sally-Dee a few months later. Ever since that time, the two of them had been inseparable.

She had drifted from town to town looking for work and a place to call her own.

Having answered an advertisement in the *Whippet Weekly* for a stable hand, Sally-Dee had been hired that very same afternoon.

It had been a difficult time. She had experienced several other tragedies in her life, which she prefers not to talk about, and which, out of respect for her privacy, I will not reveal nor dwell on. (Well, not at this stage, but maybe later if it seems relevant and advances the plot.)

The Last Lap had become her home, and the residents were

the only family she had ever known. Even her past made new friends, resulting in the two of them drifting apart. For the first time in her life, Sally-Dee could say that she belonged.

CHAPTER 3

ERNIE FROM THE BANK

"Tap, tap tap." A faint sound came from the door. Angeli limped downstairs, her face twisted in a grimace.

"Tap, tap tap." The sound grew louder.

"Hold on to your racing whippets, I'm coming as fast as me legs will go," she shouted, shuffling downstairs in her flamingo fur slippers, slightly unsteady on her feet. She was wearing tartan cotton pyjamas and a purple beanie. It was two o'clock in the afternoon, but it had been a late night. The biannual Whippet, Greyhound and Other Fast Animals Ball could be a raucous affair.

"TAP, TAP, TAP, TAP, TAP!"

Angeli reached the door, unhinged the brass latch, and creaked it open to reveal a pale man about the size of a well-fed Asian whippet.

She tilted her head down. The whippet-sized man wore light brown pants and a tweed sports coat. Small, round spectacles rested on his sharp nose, which appeared to rest on his bristly moustache. His teeth were slightly bucked, making him look more like a large mole than a whippet. He was, however, neither – a fact that an astute observer would quickly note.

"Mrs Cup?" He coughed.

"Ms Cup! Never been married. Single and fancy free." She fluffed up her brindle-coloured hair. "Ms Angeli Cup to you, but friends call me Angeli. I'm not sure what my enemies call me. They don't really call me very often or come around much." She tapped her chin with the index finger of her right hand. "I should find out, though. Something mean, I imagine. Remind me to ask Rocco what *he* calls me." She smiled the whole time she talked, revealing teeth that were perfectly symmetrical except for her left front canine, which was chipped. The reason for the chip, though not relevant to our story, was a reminder that Angeli had not always been prone to settling arguments peacefully.

"Ms Cup, I'm from the bank, I am—"

"Oh, from the *bank*," Angeli interrupted, ushering him in. "How exciting. So nice of you to drop by. I imagine it must be lovely to get out of that musty bank building and come out to the country. Do you like whippets?"

Ernie coughed again. "Er, well, no, but that's not why I'm here. The reason I am here," he continued, "is because—"

"Maybe you haven't met the right sort of whippets," Angeli interrupted again. "If you did, I'm sure you would love them – except for the Italian whippets, which can be a handful. A bit inappropriate, and too frisky, if you know what I mean," Angeli nudged Ernie with her elbow, winked her left eye, and continued, "Do you want to meet my whippets? They're not at all Italian." [1]

"Er, no. I'm here to talk about a money matter," Ernie continued.

"Oh, let me guess! Have we w-won some money?" She

---

1. *The author would like to unreservedly apologise to any Italian whippets who are offended by the racial stereotypes mentioned by Ms Cup. I will send you some pepperoni dog treats, if that helps.*

stammered with anticipation. "Oh, how exciting. I do love winning money. Well, I guess most people do, don't they? I hope it's a lot. You see, it's very expensive to run this establishment. So, how much money are we talking about?"

"How much money? Er, Ms Cup. I'm not sure what ... I mean ... I don't ... no. No, Ms Cup. I am here because—"

"Quick! Sally-Dee, Rex, Destiny," she turned and yelled. "Come over here. There's a man from the bank who says we've won so much money he doesn't know how much. I think we've won the lottery or something."

"Lottery? What l-lottery?" Ernie stammered.

"Lottery," repeated long-time porcupine resident Bugsby Pratwaffle, who had a single wispy grey spine left atop his head and a curious habit of repeating everything he heard, like a talking parrot.

Bugsby was so old and so deaf that he could only hear and hold a few words in his head at one time, at least two of which appeared to be expletives. When he spoke, Bugsby did so at a volume that made The Last Lap's whippet residents experience a sensation not unlike chalk scratching down a blackboard – if the blackboard was made of gravel and the chalk was made of chain mail. Angeli and the other residents frequently had to cut off Bugsby's squawking.

Angeli Cup turned back to the mole-like whippet-looking banker. "Do sit down, Mr ... er. What did you say your name was?"

"My name? It's Mr Buttmore, but that is not important."

"Buttmore," repeated Bugsby to Ethyl Winklepimple, who was doddering around the shared kitchen making herself a cup of tea.

"Oh, of course it is important. Everyone's name is important," Angeli confided, as she led Mr Buttmore towards a floral futon in the corner of the room. "Don't you go selling yourself short, Bernie. You are important, and so is your name.

Remember, your name is your own unique calling card. Be proud of it."

"Er, it's Ernie. Ernie Buttmore. I'm here to—"

"Oh Bernie, that's a great name. Ace McBalls, who I'm sure you know, as he's very famous, writes that your name is a window to your soul ... or was it a louvre? No, that doesn't make sense. Who would have a louvre to their souls?" She chucked. "Actually, it could have been a sliding door, now that I think of it."

"Ms Cup, it's very important for me to talk to you about this," Mr Buttmore raised his finger, trying to get her attention. It did not appear to help.

"COME OVER HERE, everyone! It's Bernie from the lottery. We are RICH," Angeli shouted, waving her hands over her head, her multicoloured fingernails making unusual patterns as they circled through the air.

"Rich," repeated Bugsby. "Fu–"

"Rich!" Angeli, learning from experience, interrupted Bugsby immediately.

Rex shuffled down the stairs, wiggling his spines excitedly. Sally-Dee arrived seconds later wearing a purple-chequered jockey's outfit and black leather knee-high riding boots, both covered with a coating of thick, sticky mud, and possibly some pizza topping, the reasons for which are not important.

"What's all the kerfuffle?" said Sally-Dee.

"We've won money! Lots of it. I think we're RICH!" Angeli declared loudly.

"Well, the th-th-thing is ..." Ernie stammered.

Destiny pitter-pattered across the timber floor and collided with the door frame. "Wallop. Yelp. Woooffff."

"Oh, Destiny, this is Vernie from the bank. He has great news."

"Er, I'm Ernie, but that's not important."

"Oh, of course it is. We've been through that already, Vernie, you need to open the sliding door to your successful future self," Angeli replied.

"Well, let's hear it then. What's the big news?" Sally-Dee implored.

"Well, we-we ..." He spread his hands out before him. "We are foreclosing on The Last Lap. You have thirty days to vacate."

Rex looked confused. Destiny continued sniffing at Ernie's pockets. And Angeli's mouth opened and closed like a turtle's.

"Vacate. Shi–" Bugsby shouted to Ethyl Winklepimple.

"Thank-you-in-advance-for-your-cooperation," Ernie rushed out in one long breath, cutting them all off. "Good day."

CHAPTER 4

THE SAUSAGE BARON OF LUMPY BOTTOM

"They are majestic creatures are they not?" The words issued from the mouth of a small, bald man in blue overalls, who was peering through a pair of black binoculars. His voice had a royal quality to it. He spoke much like a person pretending to be important might sound. How important he was, of course, was a matter of perspective.

"Yes, Boss. Absolutely," agreed a large, rotund man to his left, to whom the small bald man was very important. The small man was, after all, his employer, and jobs in Lumpy Bottom were not easy to come by.

"I love the grace and elegance. Powerful. Sleek," the bald man enthused.

"Yes, Boss. Pokerish and slick." The tall, non-bald man nodded again.

"The coat, so shiny, so soft ... so delicate."

"Yes, Boss. So, decorate, so spiny ..."

The small man lowered his binoculars and turned to stare at the larger man.

"Do you even know what I am looking at, Humperdinck, you numbungler?"

"Yes, of course. Porcupines."

"Well, no, actually."

"Er ... n-no, B-Boss?" stammered the larger man, clearly confused.

"I am looking at a pack of the most beautiful creatures alive – whippets!"

The small man passed the binoculars to the large man, who placed them right in his knapsack. The small man then placed his hands in his pockets and ambled across the field, with the large man lumbering along behind.

"What I like most about whippets is how thin and muscular they are," the small man said.

The large man nodded. "Like velvet margarine," he murmured.

About five hundred yards in front of them, twenty whippets frolicked in a paddock, eating the mushrooms, which seemed to be growing all around them.

"Did you know that whippets have no body fat, none at all?" asked the bald man.

"Yes, I loves dogs, Mr P. I *loves* to look at them. I *loves* to admire them. I *loves* to touch them. I *loves* them so much I could almost ..." The taller man's words trailed off into a grin that revealed gappy teeth.

"That will be quite enough!" The short man interrupted, giving his employee a strange look.

"Why are them dogs eating the grass, though, Boss?"

"They're not eating grass, you twit. They're eating mushrooms. Whippets love them. It's what makes them such fine racing animals."

The short man in the overalls was none other than Rocco Parmigiana, the so-called Sausage Baron of Lumpy Bottom, known as Rocco to his friends. (Well, if he had had any, one would imagine that is what they might call him.) As far as anyone could tell, everyone else called him Mr P.

Rocco was thought to be one of the richest men in the boroughs. Mr Humperdinck was not – a fact Rocco would often mention.

"I'm very rich, you know, Mr Humperdinck."

"Yes, Boss. Very, very rich."

"Do you know how rich I am, Mr Humperdinck?"

"Yes, Boss. Very extremely rich."

"No, Mr Humperdinck. In some ways, I am a very poor man. But, if my plan works, that will all change very soon."

CHAPTER 5
THE SAUSAGINATOR

Clank. Crunch. Ting. Squelch.
Clank. Crunch. Ting. Squelch.
Clank! Crunch! CRRRRRR!

Suddenly, the factory sounds were replaced with silence. Total silence. A few minutes later, a *clip-clopping* sound grew ever so steadily louder, and louder, and louder. The clopping came from the eastern corridor, from behind a green door marked, 'DO NOT ENTER. NEVER EVER. THIS MEANS YOU, TOO, MUM!'

The door opened, and a large, lumpy man emerged. "Oh, poppycock!" he muttered. "Mr P will not be pleased. Not at all very pleased. Very unpleased, I think."

He lumbered towards a large silver object, which resembled a giant upside-down toilet plunger. The Silver Toilet Plunger Thingy (STPT) was lodged in a green-looking plastic dog bowl type object (PDBTO).

The lumpy man ran his gloved hand around the base of the STPT until he reached a very particular spot. His right arm disappeared into the PDBTO. The man made a number of faint gurgling sounds. A minute or so later, his right arm reappeared holding a small brown studded collar.

“What the blazes is going on?” The unmistakeable voice of Rocco Parmigiana blurred from six large loudspeakers on the factory walls.

“Get that sausaginator going, Mr. Humperdinck! I’ve got chihuahua sausages to make!”

The lumpy man flicked the collar into the bin by the wall, walked to the STPT, and pulled a red lever marked ‘Emergency override sausage maker’. The silver plunger started to hammer up and down in its green surroundings, slowly increasing in speed.

Clank. Crunch. Ting. Squelch.

Clank. Crunch. Ting. Squelch.

A black cylindrical hose the diameter of a tennis ball flickered and undulated. It ran from the bottom side of the PDBTO to the bottom of a red door marked, ‘DO NOT EVEN THINK ABOUT COMING IN HERE, EVER. UNLESS IT’S YOU, MUM.’

The factory machines returned to their daily monotonous cacophony. Order had been restored. The lumpy man vanished behind the green door.

CHAPTER 6
THE GOLDEN CUP

Rex waddled across the wooden floor. He snuggled his back spines onto Destiny's front paw.

Destiny stayed still.

"Did he say he was taking The Last L-Lap?" Angeli stammered.

"He can't do that," Sally-Dee stated defiantly. "Can he?" She turned and stared silently at Angeli.

"Sally-Dee, I have to be honest with you." Angeli chewed her bottom lip. "I'm broke. The Last Lap is broke."

"Broke!" Bugsby shouted so loudly that Ethyl Winklepimple dropped her teacup, splattering hot liquid down the wall.

Angeli sighed.

"But I thought we were doing so well," said Sally-Dee. "We have more than fifty residents and a waiting list of more than twelve months. Our rooms are full." Sally immediately fetched the mop and began tidying up the mess.

Angeli limped over to Destiny and Rex and began hugging and stroking them. Stroking Destiny was a natural and lifelong habit, built on a shared history of love, respect and trust. Hugging Rex was an error of attention brought on by stress.

"AHHHH," Angeli screamed.

Rex looked bemused. He had no idea what had come over her. Even porcupines do not hug other porcupines. It's a bad idea all round.

Recovering from her momentary lapse of common sense, Angeli continued, "I'm afraid, Sally-Dee, that is just fifty mouths to feed."

"But don't they pay you? Don't you earn money from the residents?" Sally-Dee looked confused.

"Oh, heavens no, Sally-Dee. None of our residents have any money. And their owners do not care. I take them in so they don't end up at the sausage factory. I can't bear the thought of that."

"Sausage factory? What do you mean?" Sally-Dee looked confused.

"Rumour has it that when their racing days are over, many whippets end up as sausage meat at Rocco Parmigiana's Lumpy Bottom Meat Emporium. It's been the talk of the town for years." Angeli patted the most recent copy of the *Lumpy Bottom Examiner*, which was spread out on the breakfast bar. "Ethyl wrote in last week's 'WHAT'S UP WINKLEBUTTY?' column that they're openly selling chihuahua sausages now, isn't that right Ethyl?"

Ethyl gave a nod and tapped her nose. Destiny gave a small yelp, and Rex held her paw tightly.

Like Destiny, Ethyl Winklepimple was retired racing whippet royalty. And, like all of The Last Lap's residents, she paid a pittance for her place in the retirement home. Now, she spent her days drinking butterfly pea tea and moonlighting as an agony aunt and gossip columnist, penning a weekly column that dished the dirt on the residents of the Lower Colon Counties.

"So, how have you been able to afford to run this place if no one pays?"

"From my winnings." Angeli bobbed her head affirmingly.

"Winnings? Lotto?" Sally-Dee asked.

"No. Racing."

"*You* used to race?" Sally-Dee scratched her head, still confused.

Angeli hobbled to a set of wooden drawers in the corner of the room and pulled out a large, leather-bound scrapbook. On the cover was a coat of arms detailing two whippets jousting. The insignia read: *Rapido est excellentia.*

Angeli slowly turned the pages, revealing pictures of her and Destiny side-by-side. She turned to the middle of the scrapbook and passed it over to Sally-Dee.

It was a newspaper article from the *Whippet Weekly*, illustrated with a photograph of a very muscular-looking whippet with a young jockey beside her. Sally-Dee read aloud.

"FIVES A CHARM: DESTINY'S POO LEAVES OTHERS FOR DEAD!

"*Destiny's Poo has done it again, beating the field to win the Winklebutty Cup for a record fifth time.*"

Sally-Dee glanced down at Destiny, who wagged her tail enthusiastically. "You're Destiny's Poo? *THE* Destiny's Poo? The greatest racing whippet of all time?"

Destiny growled and nodded.

Sally-Dee tuned back to the article.

"*Riding Destiny's Poo was legendary Jockey Angeli 'Golden' Cup.*"

Sally-Dee's jaw dropped. "No! You can't be! The Golden Cup! No ... impossible!"

"Well, yes, Sally-Dee. I was Golden Cup. I was an okay whippet jockey, back in my day."

"Okay? OKAY! More like totally, completely unbeatably AWESOME!"

"Well, maybe. Made a bit of money in my hey-day, too, me

and Destiny. We won a few trophies. Travelled the world, we did. Stayed at five-star kennels in every part of the world."

"Just hold on a minute." Sally-Dee raised her voice. "You mean to tell me that in all the months I've worked here, it never occurred to you to mention that you are *the* one and only Golden Cup?"

"Well, it never really came up in conversation," Angeli replied, scratching her head.

"And how about you, Destiny? Cat got your tongue? Never occurred to you either, did it?"

Destiny shrugged, gave a long, noncommittal stretch of her hindquarters, and wandered over to Rex, who consolingly put his paw on hers.

"Besides, Sally-Dee, that is all ancient history. We all get old. Now my knees are shot, Destiny's eyes are bad, and the money ... well, that's all gone. As for The Last Lap, I guess maybe it has to retire, too." She slumped down heavily in a wicker chair, which gave its own *hmmffph* of disgust at the thought and shot out a small puff of dog hair and dust.

Sally-Dee sighed. Destiny whimpered. Rex patted Destiny's paw and gave a soft growling sound followed by a gentle squeal. The growling was the standard porcupine gesture of reassurance and support, for which Destiny was grateful. The squeal was a porcupine fart, which was accidental, and no one was grateful for it at all.

"Oh, for goodness' sake, Rex!"

CHAPTER 7

A PRICKLY PAST

Rex had not always been a troublesome porcupine. He had been born in the hamlet of Potters Crumpy, a sleepy fishing village once known for its copper industry but now renowned for its crunchy shrimp mini-donuts.

"You should eat a shrimp mini-donut!" was the catchy slogan and song that had made Potters Crumpy donuts so popular in the early seventies.

Nathaniel John Spikington Junior (known to his friends as 'Spike'), as Rex had been christened, had no interest in seafood donuts or any such worldly distractions.

"Winners win, and losers don't!" was the mantra that his father, Nathaniel John Spikington Senior, had instilled in him from birth. Winning was the only thing that mattered. Even before Rex had been born, while he was still a tiny naked puggle in his mother's womb, his father had played marching tunes to him.

Spikington Senior – like his father, Spikington the First, and his father's father, Herbert Crumble – had been a renowned professional football player and prizefighter.

"Fighting is in your blood. You are a warrior," Spikington Senior reminded his heir every day.

Unfortunately, fighting was, in fact, not in Rex's blood at all. He was not your typical boneheaded porcupine. He hated blood, the sight of which made him queasy. He also had a needle phobia and fainted at the mere idea of school immunisations. In fact, Rex was petrified of any sharp objects: knifes, knitting needles, chopsticks, scissors, and especially doctor's needles. While trypanophobia (or a needle phobia), can be embarrassing for any teenager, for a porcupine, being terrified of getting poked was a most unfortunate curse.

On an unrelated note, he also had a severe lemon phobia (lemoniphobia) and an allergy to tomatoes – the significance of which may or may not be important to the conclusion of this story.

Spike (or Rex, as he would later become known) also had no interest in sport. His great love was mathematics. Equations were beautiful to him. Quadratics, calculus, polynomials, algebra, geometry, trigonometry – he loved it all. In primary school, his first crush had been the Fibonacci Sequence.

"The sequence dictates the perfect ratio in nature. It even predicts the pattern of porcupine quills!" Young Spike Junior had excitedly declared to his father, showing him the diagram he had drawn just that morning.

Spikington Senior, however, had continued to stare at a television-shaped box at the edge of the living area and yelled, "SMASH HIS SPIKY FACE IN!" as he jumped out of his recliner and pumped one fist in the air. He was watching his all-time favourite porcupine fighter, Sugar Sharp Weasley, fight for the vacant Potters Crumpy Cruiser Weight Boxing Championship, so the only numbers he was interested in were the ones ticking over on his SmashBet app. (We would like to take this opportunity to explicitly state that we do not in any way condone gambling, of any type, unless of course we have rigged the race and know we will win ... which we would never do.)

Rex, aka Spike Junior, had simply given a high-pitched

porcupine sigh and scampered back to his room to perform some polynomial equations.

Spike Junior had used every porcupine trick in the book to avoid boxing classes. He had been the unfortunate sufferer of a cluster of rare and unusual porcupine diseases, including porcupine flu, spike protein fever, typhoid, and porcupine toe fungus.

Spike Senior was, despite his reasonably small brain by porcupine standards, starting to suspect that his son didn't even want to fight, which was a difficult thing for him to understand, since as far as he was concerned, everyone loved fighting.

Rex had confided his concerns to his mother, but her advice for any difficult matter was, "Well, when life gives you lemons you make lemonade." This advice would usually make Rex freak out and hide under the duvet for a few hours. Even the word 'lemon' sent him into a panic.

"Time for your first fight next week, Junior," Spike Senior had announced one night at the dinner table. The tri-annual sporting carnival, the Porcupine, Echidna, Hedgehog and Other Spiky Animal Games (or PEHOSA Games, as they were known) were coming up.

Spike was petrified. He knew there was no disease or affliction known to porcupine-kind that could get him out of this one. He also knew there was no way he could fight. He was a pacifist; besides, the sight of porcupine bristles raised in anger usually made him faint or throw up – sometimes both!

There was only one option.

The night before the opening of the PEHOSA games, Spike Junior packed some food, two pairs of socks, a towel, and his favourite book on calculus into his school backpack and prepared his escape.

At twelve midnight exactly, he tiptoed downstairs and out the front door. He made sure to lock the door behind him after he waddled out into the dark, starless night.

Two minutes later, he returned ... but only to check that he had locked the front door, before waddling back into the darkness, careful not to step on any cracks on the pavement. He returned three more times, but then only to lock the front door and touch the doorknob three times with each paw.

It was 1:45 am when he checked he'd locked the front door for the final time. He waddled down to the old school and then turned towards the river, headed across the railway lines, and passed the old brewery. He reached a bridge and crossed it. And there he found a signpost. To the right was Winklebutty, to the left was Lumpy Bottom, and straight ahead was Hoopersville.

Spike Junior stood there for a while, wondering what would happen to him. Would he be able to find a nice family to live with? Would his family miss him? Would he find work? Would he ever return to Potters Crumpy? Would he ever meet a girl and get married? Thousands of thoughts, and infinitesimal probabilities, swirled in his tiny porcupine head.

Eventually, he decided to go right. The sign said it was thirty-three miles to Winklebutty, so he touched it three times with each paw and started waddling. As he did so, ponderous thoughts drifted through his mind about what might await him in Winklebutty. Mostly, he wondered whether he had locked the front door of his house.

Although he did not know it at the time, Rex would not return to Potters Crumpy for a long, long time. When he did return, he would be wearing handcuffs and facing life in prison. He did not know that either.

CHAPTER 8

WINKLEBUTTY LAST NATIONAL

"WBLN *Pretorium Nostrum* – Your Money is Our Money" – were the words carved into the granite stone of the Winklebutty Last National Bank, a light-grey building that was much heavier than its colour suggested. Large marble columns adorned the imposing façade as Sally-Dee and Angeli strode through the revolving door.

Sally-Dee was trying to walk quietly, but her racing boots *clang-banged* through the corridor and echoed across the foyer. They walked perhaps fifty yards to a sign that read, 'Que here' [sic]. About twenty people stood in line in front of them. The queue moved slowly, very slowly. Not supermarket queue slowly, or even glacier slowly, but theme-park-ride-during-school-holidays slowly.

"This might take a while." Sally-Dee sighed.

"I guess it could be a good time to chat," Angeli replied. "We don't get much time to talk, seeing as we're always so busy."

Of course, that wasn't entirely true, since there isn't much to do in a retirement home for dogs and porcupines in the evenings, except read, talk, and watch TV, and they did not have a TV. Sally-Dee was also a poor reader.

Angeli loved to talk, and whenever she mentioned that she

did not get time to talk, it usually meant that a preposterously long story was about to follow. It was a reminder that it would be a good time to grab a cup of tea, some biscuits, and settle into a comfortable recliner, preparing to spend the next few hours listening to her talk. Unfortunately, Sally-Dee did not have access to any of these things at that particular moment.

Angeli was an avid reader. She had just started reading a self-help book by the excellent motivational guru Ace McBalls called *How to Be Successful Even If You Have No Talent and Everyone Thinks You're Stupid*, which was the sequel to his ground-breaking best seller *How to Hypnotise People to Stop Them Hating You*.

Angeli had just started the first chapter, so she still recalled his advice for dealing with difficult situations: pretending something different.

"You see," she began explaining to Sally-Dee. "Ace teaches you to deal with problems by pretending they don't exist, which makes them go away." She made magic wand notions with one hand and mouthed the word, "Pfffoof!"

"So, we should imagine we're in a very short queue instead, should we?" Sally-Dee retorted.

"That would be silly, wouldn't it? It is clearly a long queue, but I suppose we could pretend we're waiting to meet someone very exciting, like the Queen. You see, it makes me feel much better. You try, Sal."

Sally-Dee rolled her eyes. "I think I'll pretend to be waiting for a colonoscopy."

"You are not taking it serious—"

"—Next," a voice interrupted mid-sentence.

"What problem can I try to help you address?" The voice belonged to a grey-haired woman with a wrinkly face much like a shar pei dog.

"Well, we need some help with our home loan. You see we've had—"

"—Home loan enquires are over at the other counter." She pointed to a slightly longer queue at the opposite end of the bank.

"But we've been waiting for more than an hour." Sally-Dee scowled.

"Yes, it does seem a rather slow queue. I, however, have been at this very window since 9:30 this morning."

"But you work here."

"Exactly! For thirty-five years, I've been at this window, which is decidedly longer than your pathetic hour. So, if you'd be kind enough to push off, I can serve another dissatisfied customer. Next!"

Approximately three hours twenty-two minutes and twelve seconds later, the pair found themselves behind a large pine desk.

"I love mahogany," said the squeaky voice from behind the desk. "It reminds me of home."

"Er, looks like pine to me." Angeli gave it a tap with her knuckles for good measure.

"Oh, are you sure? Hmm ... one second," said the squeaky voice. The owner of the voice pushed a grey button on the side of the pine table and a tinted glass panel slid away to reveal a plump, bald man whose nose was slightly bent to the left, not markedly but just enough to give his face an unusual appearance. The unusual appearance it gave him was that of an average boxer who had chosen to fight someone less average than himself a few too many times. He could almost be considered handsome, in the way that someone with a bent nose might be considered handsome by someone who liked bent noses. But he could also be considered bald, red-faced, and in need of a dietician.

"Now, where were we? Angeli Cup, how good to see you again. Next time, don't wait in the line. Tell the staff to bring you straight in. After all, I think I can bend the rules for my only cousin." The bank manager winked and smiled.

"Well, you know I never bend the rules, Phil."

"Yes, yes. I should have worked that out by now. And who is your delightful friend?" He smiled and winked at Sally-Dee.

"I'm Sally-Dee. Sally-Dee Pickles. And you are ...?" She did not wink, and her tone was whatever the opposite of delightful is.

"I'm Phillip Schiessenburger, but please call me Phil."

"Okay, I'll call you Phil, but only because I can't pronounce your last name." Sally-Dee threw the foreclosure notice on the table. "What's all this about, then?"

Phil picked up the paper, slid on his reading glasses, and began mumbling to himself as he typed on the computer. "Hmm ... ohhh... ohhh... hmm." He peered over the top of his spectacles at Angeli. "I'm sorry, Angeli, but it looks like we are going to have to repossess The Last Lap. According to our records, you haven't made repayments for more than twelve months."

"We have the money." Sally-Dee pulled out a ragged brown purse and emptied it on the pine desk. It's 398 shillings – all my savings."

Phil pushed a few of the antiquated coins around with one finger. "I'm afraid that won't quite do."

"But it's all I have. Besides, that's three months' rent for me," Sally-Dee protested.

"I'm afraid I will need the full amount owing – two thousand shillings – by the end of next month, or I won't have a choice. Sorry, Angeli. You were a great jockey once, but it's time to move on. Rules are rules, after all."

"But what about the dogs and porcupines?" Angeli pleaded. "They have nowhere else to go?"

"Well, I think I know someone who might be interested in buying them. He would pay you a good price, of course."

"You can't be serious!" Angeli replied.

Phil looked sternly at her but remained silent.

"He certainly looks serious," Sally-Dee interrupted. "Doesn't he?" Judging emotions was not her strength, so she had to take Angeli's word for it.

Phil continued to look serious. Angeli continued to look annoyed. Sally-Dee continued to look confused.

"Look, Angeli, I hate the idea as much as you do. And I know the history between you and Rocco. Unfortunately, we have to be realistic. The Last Lap is broke. I can't lend you any more money or extend you any favours without the retirement home turning an income, so unless you can think of another way to come up with two thousand shillings by the end of the next month, I'm afraid Rocco will get his hands on your farm, one way or another."

CHAPTER 9
YOU CAN'T EVEN BUTTER YOUR TOAST WITHOUT COPPER

Lumpy Bottom was the kind of town you moved to if you were old and ready to retire, or if you wanted to lay low for a while to avoid undue attention from the police or the tax office. Rocco Parmigiana was not that old, so I will let you draw your own conclusions.

Lumpy Bottom had been established as a gambling town just south of Winklebutty, due north of the Scrumpy–Potter River. Earl Winklebutt, while out looking for the incredibly rare hairy-breasted mountain tit (*Parus areolapilosa*), had instead stumbled across exotic truffles in the mountain regions of what was, at that stage, considered to be a desolate, unnamed wilderness. Profiteers from all over the country streamed to the place Winklebutt had discovered to make their fungus fortune. While they got rich in the place colloquially known as Winklebutt, they spent most of their coin in Lumpy Bottom, which became a Mecca for gambling, dancing, exotic cheeses and cheap beer.

Eventually, a tourist marketing campaign added a 'y' to the end of the town's name. "Y not come to Winklebutty?" had been a complete marketing failure as a tourist campaign, but most of the locals agreed that the 'y' made their town sound much more respectable, so they kept it.

When the fungus rush ended, many of the prospectors moved over the mountains, seeking other sources of wealth. On the banks of the Scrumpy–Potter River they struck gold – figuratively, not literally. In fact, they had found copper, which was less glamorous than its precious metal cousin but still valuable, nonetheless.

"You can live without gold, but you can't even butter your toast without copper," Earl Winklebutt would often remark. And so, the Copper Rush of '93 saw thousands of fortune hunters flock to the banks of the metal-rich Scrumpy–Potter River. Due to a typing error brought on by sleep deprivation and heat stroke, the town itself was subsequently named Potters Crumpy.

The fortune hunters of Potters Crumpy were far from the footloose, adventurous types who had augured the 1888 Winklebutty Fungus Rush. These were sensible, hard-working folk attracted to the promise of slightly above-average wages and a good health plan.

So, Potters Crumpy grew moderately from the prosperity copper brought. Earl Winklebutt Junior continued the family copper business, passing it on to his son, Earl Winklebutt the Third, who passed it to his son, Rockingham Winklebutt. Rockingham had spent all his life in Winklebutt until, through a series of humorous misadventures, he chanced upon nearby Lumpy Bottom. What he saw would change not only his own destiny but that of the whole region.

Rockingham saw the bright neon lights, the music halls, and the gambling venues all set amid lush bushes abundant with great tits (*Parus major*). Compared to Potters Crumpy, Lumpy Bottom was a metropolis – a bustling city full of adventure, a thriving den of recklessness built on the solid wealth of copper. The sensible accountants and stockbrokers lived and worked in

Winklebutty, but they delighted in and partied in Lumpy Bottom.

Here, there were delicious foods of all descriptions – pastries, cakes, chocolates and hamburgers – every delicacy Rockingham could imagine, and many that he could not.

Rockingham Winklebutt was hooked. Although he was not interested in copper, he fell in love with food.

❧

At first, Rocco began experimenting with caviar, oysters and other fishy delights. Then, he began making cheeses. Rockingham immediately sold the family copper factory and bought an old storage shed in the centre of the new city, changing his name to the more exotic-sounding Rocco Parmigiana and becoming the largest cheesemaker in the district. A short time after, his main competitor, Albertonio Gorgonzola, the proprietor of Albertonio's Stinky Cheese Bazaar, disappeared, and his factory unexpectedly blew up for no obvious reason at all.[1]

Later, when Rocco got bored with cheeses, sausages became his passion. He became obsessed with them, but not just any old bratwursts; these would be the best-ever sausages in the whole of the Lower Colon Counties. His emporium would be the Mount Everest of the sausage-making industry, except not as high or as cold or as hard to get to.

And so began Rocco's sausage empire. At first, he started selling small frankfurters and cheerios, but he soon moved on to saveloys and hotdogs. As the popularity of his sausages grew, so did their size and complexity.

Rocco's passion for cured meats became all-consuming. He

---

1. *For legal reasons, the author would like to clarify that there is no implication Mr Parmigiana was in any way linked to this unfortunate tragedy.*

started buying up rival sausage businesses. If the owners did not want to sell ... well, let's just say that Rocco was a persuasive negotiator; so persuasive that, in time, he became known as the Sausage Baron of Lumpy Bottom, the most successful spiced meat merchant in the county.

And there, in Lumpy Bottom's main street, Sausagecopper Lane, stood his legacy: a large oblong building, four stories tall and as large as a football field but with only one discernible window. A towering red-brick chimney rose from the northern side of the building, belching out a steady plume of speckled smoke.

A bumper-to-bumper flow of grey-and-white trucks passed through the metal doors of the north side and exited from the west. And across the eastern entrance, in large capital letters each the size of a fully grown puggle, were the words:

ROCKINGHAM SAUSAGE FACTORY
MAKING LUMPY BOTTOM GREAT AGAIN

CHAPTER 10
YOU WILL NOT BE BEATEN

Angeli puttered across the pine floor, muttering incomprehensibly to herself as she refilled the dish soap in the communal kitchen–dining area. She had been muttering since her meeting with Phil Schiessenburger, and based on her past behaviour, she was likely to continue to do this indefinitely unless Sally-Dee intervened.

"She's been like this all week," Sally-Dee confided to Rex, who was sitting with Ethyl Winklepimple and some of The Last Lap's other decrepit residents, helping them play Sudoku. "Ever since we went to the bank."

Rex just scratched his side bristles, indicating that he shared her concerns, and also that he had a stubborn case of porcupine fleas.

Porcupine fleas, I should add, are a particularly bad-tempered, more robust version of their canine counterparts. They are well-adapted to the inhospitable environment of porcupine bristles, which are nowhere near as accommodating as dog hair.

In nature, whippets and porcupines are sworn enemies, never associating except during periods of drought or conflict. In the wild, gangs of porcupines track unsuspecting whippets, waiting until they're asleep to leap on them in a game they call 'Whippet Pincushion'. Whippets are understandably unimpressed by these shenanigans. In response, they travel in hunting packs, finding porcupines and barking at them with their ultrasonic high-pitched squeals. Porcupines are so sensitive to these sounds that they'll do anything to escape, even jumping into raging rivers.

Porcupines, of course, are not strong swimmers and they are especially bad at freestyle, backstroke, and butterfly. By an ironic twist of fate, they are not too bad at doggy paddle, but they still detest water.

To a whippet, the sight of a distressed porcupine lolling around in a freezing, fast-flowing river, its paws flapping around like tiny, useless propellers, is especially amusing. And thus, whippets and porcupines have coexisted for generations in a tense, never-ending game of canine-and-hystricomorpha rivalry. This accepted natural order remained until Angeli Cup threw caution to the wind and brought Mother Nature's sworn foes together at The Last Lap.

It had been difficult at first. All the experts told her it could not be done, that porcupines and whippets could never coexist. "It would be like housing lions with zebras, or snakes with mice, or fish with donkeys," zoologists had insisted.

Angeli had ignored the mutterings and misgivings of her detractors, not because she was stubborn and pig-headed, however – nor because she was certain she could succeed – but purely because she was quite hard of hearing.

Decades of whippet-racing had left her tone deaf to certain frequencies in at least one ear.

All the whippet yelping was not the cause. Whippets are, unless provoked by porcupines, a very quiet breed of dog and their very singular, specific ultrasonic high-frequency yelp is reserved for porcupine baiting. It is something like the frequency of music made by the Bee Gees.

When galloping, whippets are particularly quiet, not at all like their clumsy racing cousins, the greyhounds. The noise of whippet racing has been described as similar to the sound of two small ornamental pillows colliding rapidly with a great big pillow, or of parmesan cheese being firmly squeezed in anger.

Exposure to this sound over so many years of racing, along with the roars of the crowds, had left Angeli unable to hear certain low-pitched noises, such as the grunts made by the singer Tom Jones or the sound of sperm whales alerting their pod to danger. (On an unrelated note, this unfortunate selective hearing loss had once almost resulted in calamity on a snorkelling trip to the Bahamas.)

The main cause of Angeli's deafness, however, was entirely self-inflicted. It was caused by her constantly shouted words of encouragement when she was riding Destiny's Poo.

Angeli Cup was a gentle soul who detested using a whip on her dog. Despite their name, whippets rarely require or enjoy whipping. So, from her twenties onwards, Angeli only wore a whip for ornamental purposes, looking every bit the part of a professional with her whip and thigh-high black leather riding boots. Instead, she would yell constant encouragement in her dog's ear.

"Go, girl! You will *not* be beaten. You *can't* lose! You *cannot* fail. You will *not give up*!" Angeli had used these words so many times that she was now selectively deaf to the words 'can't', 'lose', 'not' and 'give up'.

Sally-Dee had learnt to use alternate words, ones that Angeli could hear, to get around this problem. So, when all of Angeli's financial advisors had told her, in their own words, to, "*Give up!* Your idea of The Last Lap will *not* work. You should definitely *not* invest everything you've ever won. You *can't* win with this venture!" All Angeli heard was a faint hum, a squelch, and the words, "Your idea of The Last Lap ... will work. You should definitely ... invest everything you've ever won. You ... win with this venture!" And that had been Angeli's driving force: an underlying belief in herself that she could not fail. And she never did.

All she could hear in her head were the words, "There is always a way!"

And there always was ... until now.

CHAPTER 11

USUALLY, MOST OF THE TIME

"I have an idea." Sally-Dee marched across to the mahogany table where Rex and Destiny were having breakfast and slapped the latest issue of the *Lumpy Bottom Examiner* down on the table.

The headline read, "**HER CUP RUNNETH DRY. LAST LAP TO CLOSE AS BANKERS CLOSE IN**".

"A special report by The Last Lap's own Ethyl Winklepimple," Angeli read, craning her neck to read the words and enunciating each one. She frowned at Ethyl, who simply shrugged and returned to her truffle breakfast mash.

Rex glanced at the paper and looked apprehensive. He did not like the headline, but he also very often did not like Sally-Dee's ideas. Last month, for instance, Sally-Dee's idea had been that porcupine bristles could be used to make cheap and effective brushes.

Rex had assumed she meant hairbrushes and was delighted that his bristles might be used to brush all the whippets. Firm but forgiving, porcupine quills are often used by high-end hairdressers in the very best hairbrushes. It was only later, and slightly too much later to avoid most of the unpleasantries, that Rex had discovered Sally-Dee meant toilet brushes.

Even that might not have been quite as significant an issue if it were not for the difficulty of removing bristles from porcupines. Porcupine spines are firmly embedded under the skin and are almost impossible to remove without strong chemical reagents or high-voltage electricity. Both systems are very effective and well-tolerated by everyone except for the porcupine, which, in this case, was almost exclusively Rex.

After many futile attempts, Sally-Dee eventually abandoned her business plan. But Rex was still undergoing physical therapy to encourage his bodily scars to heal. As for his emotional scars, well, it's hard to tell whether they'll ever improve. To this day, he remains unable to tolerate the sound of a hairdryer without having uncontrollable seizures.

"We're going to win the Winklebutty Cup and save The Last Lap!" Sally-Dee declared triumphantly, and somewhat prematurely.

This time, as you can imagine, Rex was glad to hear that Sally-Dee's plan did not involve any suffering on his part. In time, that would turn out to be significantly incorrect, and would, demonstrably, be another error of judgment on Rex's part, but at that precise moment, Sally-Dee's suggestion that Destiny and Angeli try to win the next Winklebutty Cup seemed like a perfectly reasonably idea.

It was not, of course, an idea that was likely to succeed, but it was an idea that was less likely to result in the kind of permanent injuries Rex had incurred from Sally-Dee's last flight of fancy.

"You see! Rex thinks it's a great idea!" Sally-Dee announced, pointing to the rapid undulation of Rex's lower tummy spines.

He was actually signalling that he needed to pee, which Sally-Dee may or may not have known.

Destiny was also surprised by Rex's attitude to the plan, given that she also had several reservations. After all, she and Angeli Cup had been in retirement for almost five years. Neither was in any shape to walk briskly, let alone run. Plus, Angeli had lost most of her sight, some of her hearing, and had arthritis in her elbows, knees, and nose. Destiny was also totally out of shape and had become rather used to overeating and under-exercising. Most importantly, however, and unknown to everyone except two other people, was the most significant reason why Destiny could no longer race.

Just as Destiny was about to raise this issue with Sally-Dee – after all, it was a significant issue that would make racing foolhardy and potentially dangerous – she stopped, scratched her left teat third from the top contemplatively, and thought about it for a minute.

She was *going* to say something. She was *going* to raise her objections. She was *going* to make it perfectly clear to everyone why it would be foolishly ill-advised for her to sprint ever again. Then, she looked at Rex, who was still moving his spines in an uncomfortable kind of way, and thought, *Well, if Rex thinks I can race, I will damn well race. Thank you, Rex, for giving me the confidence to overcome my fear and get back under the saddle to save The Last Lap.*

Rex stared back up at her. He had no idea what she was thinking, or why she was eyeballing him in that weird way while scratching her abdomen. He thought the idea of Destiny racing again was daft, while still better than Sally-Dee's last few ideas. And now he really, really needed to pee.

Sally-Dee raised her right fist in the air in an awkward gesture of confirmation. "So, it is decided. We *are* going to save The Last Lap by winning the Winklebutty Cup this year. Angeli Cup and Destiny will race, and me and Rex will train them."

CHAPTER 12

EVERYTHING RIDES ON HER

Rex stood defiantly, his face unemotional. He was wearing a white Gi and black Akami pants. Around his waist was a black ribbed-cotton belt, indicating that he was a practitioner of the Japanese martial art of Aikido.

"Arrghhh" Rex gargled as he flew through the early morning air and landed gracelessly on a bamboo mat with a soft *plonk*.

"Oh, Rex! Are you even trying? That's ten nil to Destiny. You're a black belt after all," Angeli scolded.

A few feet in front of him Destiny stood wagging her tail in a gentle, pendular rhythm. She had not yet raised a sweat.

Rex waddled back to the bench and sat down. He was too winded to reply.

In fact, Rex was not a real black belt and had not attended any martial arts training. He had, however, discovered an ingenious way to dye his belt different colours to fool his father into thinking he was attending his martial arts gradings.

Ordinarily, Rex was opposed to any sort of violence. He was, however, determined to help Destiny train for the race. He was willing to compromise his principles and break a few bristles for the greater good.

"Four weeks to the cup," Angeli mumbled to herself, gesturing towards Destiny. Time to lose those pounds. We need to get you race fit."

Destiny let out a faint, despondent growl.

It had been five years since Destiny raced, which is about 5.5 whippet years, 6.1 porcupine years and 4.2 elephant years. The five-time winner of the Winklebutty Cup's hunger for victory and glory had long been replaced by her hunger for spicy Indian curries and afternoon naps. No longer was she the most feared dog in whippet racing.

Most days, her victories seemed to belong to a different dog. Now, her knees were stiff, her eyes were poor, and her confidence was shot. Destiny knew the seriousness of her situation. Everything was riding on her, quite literally. She had four weeks to train to win the most coveted race in the whippet-racing calendar or they would all lose their home.

The thing was, she was no longer the only five-time winner. Destiny would now be racing against the new, most-feared, most-admired whippet in racing – the formidable racer Fate's Fur Art.

Destiny pushed the thoughts aside and started her training regime. Up at 4 am, weightlifting, stretching, Tai Chi, and calisthenics. After lunch, martial arts: Aikido and Jiujitsu. In the evening, she did cross-fit, pilates and pliability training. Then, to bed at 9 pm on the dot, right after a sneaky glass of port or sherry, all to be back up at four the next morning. Happily, Rex was there with her every step of the way. Well, not quite every step, but a reasonable amount of the time, and especially for the glass of port and the stretching. During the training, he much preferred to support Destiny from afar, offering encouraging words and porcupine grunts while he read 'WHAT'S UP WINKLEBUTTY?' in the *Examiner* and drank espresso coffee.

Angeli Cup was also doing her best to get into shape. It felt so much harder than it used to when she was younger. But she pushed through the pain, the early morning wake-ups, the regimented diet, and the afternoon dark beer. The beer wasn't part of the training plan, but she had bribed Rex into turning a blind eye to her occasional slip-ups. Sally-Dee, however, was not so forgiving.

After a couple of weeks, the training regime was starting to take its toll on Angeli Cup's body. She loved the discipline and the pain of the rigorous training. It wasn't the physical pain that was the problem. Mentally however, she was struggling.

Each time she pulled on her racing britches, it triggered memories of the 112th Winklebutty Cup, which all came flooding back to her ... the one memory that haunted Angeli 'Golden' Cup to this day. The one act for which she could never ever, ever, forgive herself.

She glanced at Destiny, and then at Sally-Dee, and her lip quivered. Suddenly, Angeli felt an emotion she had never felt before. Her stomach churned with a thousand large African butterflies, and her hands trembled like cold baby quolls.

She felt fear – and possibly some heartburn or indigestion. She was not a qualified doctor, so it was very hard for her to be certain.

CHAPTER 13
THE WHIPPET WHISPERER

Angeli waddled across the kitchen, much the way a porcupine with a severe case of porcupine fleas waddles. She did not, however, have porcupine fleas, which was confusing for Rex who had earlier in the day decided to help her by pouring rancid mayonnaise on her clothes while she slept.

Rex was not a qualified veterinarian, nor was he a qualified pest control expert, but this, of course, was widely recognised as the most effective treatment for porcupine fleas.

Strangely, it did not seem to help Angeli's issue at all.

"You look awful," observed Sally-Dee. "And you smell like off Caesar Salad."

"Long story. I don't feel too flash," Angeli said, brushing a smear of mayo off the knickerbockers she preferred to race in. "Sally-Dee, the truth is, I can't race. I'm too old, too slow, too ... well, too ...everything!"

"How long?" Sally-Dee quizzed her.

"How long what?"

"This story, how long is it? You see, I can only hang around until lunchtime, and then I have to go into town to do shopping and pay the bills. By my calculations, I can spare one and a half hours maximum. Maybe you could split your story into two parts if it's longer than that."

"Er, that was the story. I'm injured, and I can't race, so you will have to race in my place. Oh, and someone poured rancid mayonnaise on me while I slept. No idea who that was."

"It was Rex. But anyway. No, I can't race. *You* have to race. *You're* Golden Cup, not me."

"No Sally-Dee, I *was* Golden Cup. Now, I'm more like Copper Goblet or maybe Ceramic Mug. I can't race. And why would Rex pour mayonnaise on me?"

"Er, you can be whatever mug you want, but you HAVE to race. Rex thinks you have porcupine fleas."

Angeli stood motionless, her mouth slightly ajar and her eyes flicking from side to side as she tried to process what was happening. By that stage, Rex and Destiny had arrived.

"I'm so sorry, Destiny, but I have to be honest with you. I can't do it. I just can't. My body is too old, too slow," Angeli lied. Her body was still strong, and her mind was sharp, but her heart was gone. She had lost the passion to compete.

"But you have to. Without the prize money from the win, we'll lose The Last Lap."

"I know, but ..."

"You're just going to give up?" Sally-Dee tapped her foot in frustration. "You're just going to let the bank or Rocco take our home? What about all the whippets and porcupines who rely on you? Someone has to fight for them. Destiny can't do this without you."

Destiny turned her head and half lifted her tail. She turned toward Sally-Dee. She didn't say a word. She did not need to.

"No, no. No, no, no, and no again! I know what you are thinking ..." Sally-Dee replied. "I'm not a jockey! I've never raced before."

"But you ride the dogs every day – every one of them. And

they love you and think you're the best jockey ever," Angeli replied.

"Do they say that? Do they say I'm the best?" Sally's green eyes lit up.

Strictly speaking, none of the whippets had ever said that. In fact, there was a general consensus among the whippets that Sally-Dee was an extremely bad rider. It was not that she didn't try or lacked enthusiasm. It was mainly that she was so insecure and needy.

Instead of reassuring the dogs and telling them how good they were doing, Sally-Dee would constantly ask for feedback. "Am I doing okay? Oh God, I'm awful, aren't I? I'm such a bad jockey!" These questions would result in the whippets having to spend a lot of time reassuring Sally-Dee that it wasn't her fault they hadn't been able to run a lap in a minute, or that her parents *and* her pet hamster had died.

Of course, the dogs had become very used to ignoring Sally-Dee's pity party, instead making reassuring grunts and snuffles in the appropriate places.

This moment, however, was not the time for truth-telling. Sally-Dee was in no frame of mind to deal with the truth (least of all being that she was very much at fault for the death of her hamster, since hamsters are not at all well designed for rocket flight).

Angeli Cup did what any self-respecting jockey and property owner would do: she lied through her false teeth. "The dogs love you. They say you inspire them. They call you the Whippet Whisperer!" Angeli worried that she had overdone it with that last fib.

Luckily, Sally-Dee was too emotional to detect even obvious signs of fabrication. "Do they *really* say that? They call me the Whippet Whisperer?"

"Yes, of course. You tell her, Destiny."

Destiny did not want to be dragged into this web of deceit.

Besides, it is almost impossible for whippets to lie, as their tails tend to shake uncontrollably when they do – just one of the reasons whippets are not good at games of chance, such as poker or running for a political position. But Destiny knew that if she did not lie, their hopes of saving The Last Lap would end. She had to convince Sally-Dee that she was a fantastic jockey, rather than the incompetent jockey she really was.

"Tell her, Destiny. She's a great jockey, isn't she?" Angeli pleaded with her. It was a gamble, but she had nothing to lose.

All eyes were on Destiny. She stared into Sally-Dee's eyes and nodded affirmatively. Everyone watched Destiny's tail. Any tiny quiver, shake or vibration would be seen as a sign of dishonesty. Destiny's tail stayed firm, strong, and upright, with not a sign of hesitancy.

"Well, Destiny, if you believe in me, I will believe in myself. I'll race."

"Great! Let's start training." Angeli took Sally-Dee out to the stables. As she left, Rex removed the spine he had carefully jabbed into Destiny's hindquarters at a very specific acupuncture point – the only part of Destiny's derrière that still had any feeling. As soon as he removed it, the nerve started to function again. Destiny's tail immediately collapsed and started to wag faster than a racing whippet's heartbeat.

She had, of course, been lying through her very real canine teeth.

Sally-Dee was an awful jockey, but in modern whippet racing that didn't really matter. Whippets could race faster and better without a jockey. The only reason they continued to have a human ride them was that the viewing audience preferred it. Having jockeys created more tension and excitement, especially if there was a crash. Otherwise, jockeys were totally useless and only slowed the dogs down. Some dogs communicated directly with the trainers, who gave them their racing instructions by radio-transmitter earpiece. All the jockeys had to do was hang on and not get in the way.

Sally-Dee did not fully understand this aspect of racing. She did not know that she had been chosen to ride only because she was small and light, the ideal features of a whippet jockey. All she had to do in the race was not fall off, let Destiny do the running, and not talk too much.

Over the next month, Sally-Dee trained every day. She did riding drills, jumping drills, and evasion drills. She studied the history of not just whippet racing but also every type of animal racing in the history of racing sports. None of that would influence the outcome of the race in the slightest way, but it kept her busy and out of harm's way.

When race day came, Sally would be totally ready to fulfil her duty as a whippet jockey and do what she was destined to do – stay thin and not fall off until Destiny crossed the finish line.

Unfortunately, Sally-Dee was not aware of Destiny's problem. If she had known, she would almost certainly never have agreed to ride.

CHAPTER 14
CHATTANOOGA CHAD

"So nice of you to make it." Rocco waved his arms in a welcoming gesture of sorts.

"Glad to help," replied a tall young man with a mild lisp and a cowlick.

"Humperdinck." Rocco gestured to his henchman. "I'd like you to meet my nephew, Chad Cheerio."

"Oooh," Mr Humperdinck stated, which was not what he meant or planned to say. He had hoped to say something clever or witty to impress his racing idol. Instead, he mumbled, "So, youse are Chattanooga Chad."

"You've heard of me, I gather. Of course you have! Who hasn't? Five-time winner of the Winklebutty Cup and three times Dog and Marsupial Jockey of the Year, but don't be intimidated. I'm just an ordinary guy who's super-talented, attractive, rich and popular. Just call me Chad."

"It's s-such an honour, C-Chad," Mr Humperdinck stammered.

"On second thoughts, call me Mr Cheerio."

"Of course, Mr Cheerio," grovelled Humperdinck.

"Or maybe call me Mr Chad Chevrolet."

"Of course, Mr Chevrolet," repeated Humperdinck. "Sounds very proper and important."

"Let's get on with it," Rocco interrupted. "Do you have the parcel?"

Chad nodded and winked his left eye. He gestured for Rocco to follow him outside. A small van with blue stripes was parked on the pebbled driveway. Chad unlocked the rear door and slid it open.

Inside was a dark box with vertical metal bars. Behind the bars stalked a shadowy figure. It was hard for Rocco to make out the details in the dim light, but it looked something like a very big, mottled whippet-like thing.

"That, my dear uncle, is the guaranteed unbeatable winner of this year's Winklebutty Cup," Chad elaborated. "That is Fate's Fur Art."

Mr Humperdinck again made an 'Oooooh' type of sound.

"Fate's Fur Art is the most famous whippet in racing history. Five-time winner of the Cup, tied with Destiny's Poo. He is soon, however, to be the only ever six-time winner," Chad boasted.

"How can youse be so sure 'e'll win?" Mr Humperdinck asked. "The *Examiner* 'as reported Destiny's Poo 'as come out of retirement to race. There's some ovva speedy dogs, too. Gonna be a tight race."

Chad strode up to the box with the steel bars and banged on them twice. The shadowy figure prowled towards them. As it came into the light, it was possible to see its yellow and black spots and curved bushy tail. It had a round face and an unmistakeable purr."

"That's no whippet! That's ... er ... that's a ... ch-cheetah!" Humperdinck stuttered.

"Well, yes! It may look like that right now, but with a bit of grey paint and some throat spray to stop him purring, no one will tell the difference. I mean, they haven't so far, have they?" Chad glanced sideways at Mr Humperdinck and winked.

Chad and Rocco chuckled simultaneously.

Mr Humperdinck looked confused. “But you ’as gots to be a whippet to race in the Cup?”

“Exactly! That’s why we will paint this cheetah to look like a whippet. Understand?”

Humperdinck didn’t understand at all. “But, Boss, is that not cheating?”

“That, Mr Humperdinck, my dear friend, is precisely *why* he is called a cheetah!”

Then the three men started chuckling all together.

Two of them had a devious plan. One of them did not. He had no idea why he was laughing and just wanted to feel like part of the group.

CHAPTER 15
DESTINY'S DESTINY

Destiny had not always been the GOAT of whippet racing. In school, by whippet standards she was tall, very shy, and as socially awkward as wooden underpants. But give her a mathematical problem and she was in her element.

Numbers she loved: evens, odds, real, unreal ones. Destiny loved all of them, except for twelve. She hated the number twelve even more than she hated the number seven.

Twelve just felt *wrong*. The way that eating ice cream before dinner felt wrong. The way that wearing no clothes felt wrong, at least if you weren't a whippet. The way wearing clothes back to front and inside out felt wrong. Twelve was stupid.

Why, she thought to herself, *would you have twelve months in a year, with a variable number of days in each month, and then seven days in the week?* Don't even get me started on how much Destiny hated having seven days in each week. *Why seven, besides arbitrarily interpreted religious texts?*

If Destiny had her way, there would be eighteen months in each year, ten days in each week, and twenty days in each month, which would be much more understandable and reasonable. She had tried to explain this to her teachers at school, but they were having none of it. They said something about a religious book, some kind of decree there should only be seven days, and they should rest on the seventh. Well for one thing, there were never any rest days for her, so that made no sense at all.

In early high school, Destiny had amazed her teachers by solving one of mathematics most long-standing problems – Fermat's Dilemma – using only prime numbers, two dog biscuits, and a piece of mouldy cheese. In mathematics class, she was in her element, having memorised pi to 350 decimal places.

Talking to boys, however, was not one of her skills. Parties and social events were a nightmare for her. Destiny could not make small talk. She had no idea how to pick up on social cues of any sort – and, for a dog, that was really saying something. Unfortunately, she couldn't even interpret the meaning of a wagging tail!

Now, to humans a wagging tail might seem an obvious sign of excitement or happiness. For whippets, however, there are infinite nuances to the meaning and mood of tail wags. It depends on the frequency, tone, firmness and positioning of the tail. Short frequencies with a high tail lift usually mean interest and curiosity, while a slight lean and a frantic whipping of the tail can mean condescending sarcasm. A low, rapid wag means deception, while a side wag usually just means a tail cramp. Nearly all of these nuances completely eluded poor Destiny. She had mostly been able to overcome the problem by learning about social skills and the subtleties of tail wagging from language picture books.

Ace McBalls, the self-described 'Grandmaster of Confidence', in his audio book series *Wag Hard: Be Hard,* had taught her the importance of confident doggy language.

"Your tail is your destiny," he repeated in his podcasts. "Always point your tail to your destiny, to the heavens and beyond!"

With the help of Ace McBalls, Destiny had been able to learn how to walk, talk, growl, and bark like a confident dog.

"Shake it until you fake it!" Ace always insisted. Destiny practiced her tail wags in front of the mirror until she learnt the twelve major whippet wags off by heart.

Unfortunately, she was never able to learn the importance of dog scent and odour. Smells are even more complicated for dogs than tail movements. Some odours mean happiness, others mean anger, and yet others indicate that you forgot to bathe that morning. Destiny had no idea how to interpret any of them, and less than no idea on how to create the correct scent for the correct occasion.

For a whippet, this was a huge problem.

Whippets are dogs of few words. They can talk if they want to, but they always don't because they can say so much more with a smell than they can with words. 'Say it with stank!' was the slogan of the most popular canine perfume in Winklebutty: Kennel Number 5.

Not only could Destiny not understand odours, but to be honest, she wasn't really into sniffing other dogs' butts. She preferred her nose cold, moist, and a reasonable distance away from another dog's bottom or a pile of poop on the sidewalk.

"What do you mean you don't like the smell of crap? Every dog loves smelling stinky things. That's what we *do*! We're dogs for goodness' sakes," was the less-than-supportive reaction she received from her father when she first mentioned she did not really like smells – at least not all smells.

She enjoyed the aromas of candy and rose petals; these, however, were not the sort of objects her family liked to sniff.

Destiny's olfactory peculiarities were an ongoing source of tension in her household until she decided to leave home and follow her racing dream.

CHAPTER 16

THE 'POO-CUP' PAIR

Destiny's birthname was Abigail Gertrude Frankenfarter. Her father was a German Shepherd and the fourteenth in line to the throne of the Kingdom of Weinercrump. Her mother was an Italian greyhound from the bad side of the Upper Plains. Their romance and marriage had created quite a scandal in the district. After all, who would have thought that Archduke Felix Frankenfarter would elope with a common *corgi* from the Italian Alps. Still, no one could doubt the radiance and canine beauty of Princess Sophia Lasagna.

To avoid constant media scrutiny, the regal couple had run off to the farthest place they could find.

They took twelve suitcases, three cases of champagne, and their designer sunglasses and bought two first class tickets on the *Destiny of the Waves* – the largest, most opulent cruise ship in the world.

Three weeks later, they docked at the port of Potters Crumpy.

Abigail was born nine weeks later.

Unfortunately, the fairytale romance did not last. Sophia tired of the simple life. She had been swept of her feet by the romance and excitement of a princely courtship, and a simple country life was not for her. She left before Abigail's first birthday.

Felix did the best he could as a single father, but he missed his homeland, and he began to drink heavily. Money was tight, so Abigail decided to work at the racing stables. The hours were long, and the pay was poor. It was there, however, that fate would change her life. There, she met a young up-and-coming jockey.

"My name's Angeli. What's your name?" Angeli had asked, and from there, the friendship bloomed.

"Now, you need a racing name, you know," Angeli told her. "Abigail is not really much of a racing name, is it?"

Abigail hadn't thought about it.

"You see, names are *very* important. Your racing name must represent your inner drive, your purpose, how you got here and where you are going."

Abigail recalled the story her mother had told her about how they had sailed to Potters Crumpy on *Destiny of the Waves*.

"That's a nice name. But you can't just copy a name. It has to be your own. What's your destiny, Abigail?"

At that moment, the owner of the stables had walked in. "Come on, Abigail. Time to clean up the stables."

"I guess your Destiny is poo," Angeli Cup chuckled, and the two of them had laughed together.

That morning, a lifelong friendship was forged, and Abigail changed her racing name to Destiny's Poo.

They did not know it yet, but the pair would go on to form the greatest racing team of the century. Over the following years, they would win more races than any other racing duo, trio, or even quartet. In fact, neither of them would ever race with anyone else.

The jockey would become known as Angeli 'Golden' Cup – the greatest mount of the modern whippet-racing era. And Destiny would go on to even greater accolades, being rated by *Animal Racing Monthly* as the greatest racing whippet of the age.

They were so close that the press and media would affectionately label their pairing the 'Poo–Cup'. In the history of whippet racing, their dominance would never, ever be challenged ... until now.

CHAPTER 17

THE RACE THAT SIGNIFICANTLY SLOWS THE COUNTIES

The precise origins of the Winklebutty Cup, and indeed whippet racing itself, are shrouded in folklore and mystery.

The Fungus Rush of 1888 brought great wealth but also great troubles to the region. And where there is money, soon afterward crime, corruption, and jealousy tend to follow.

By the 1890s, the rival towns of the county were gripped by civil unrest, and the prospect of all-out war seemed very real. Traditionally, local rivalries were resolved by the time-honoured tradition of goat steeplechase racing.

The Biannual Goat Eisteddfod brought together the feuding families and businesspeople of the region. Amid the passionate excitement that only goat steeplechase racing can create, local rivalries were forgotten, old grievances were resolved, and peace was restored to the region.

Unfortunately, the winter of 1892 was one of the coldest and longest on record. The crops failed, the cows died, and food soon ran out. The mushrooms of the region, which were excellent food sources, had been almost wiped out by the fungus spraying campaign.

Desperate and hungry, the locals of Lumpy Bottom Plains

had little option but to eat their beloved steeplechase goats. Even Leaping Lorelle, the greatest steeplechase goat of the modern era, found herself on the wrong side of a boiling pot of mutton.

That year, there would be no steeplechase.

The locals grew restless and angry. The mayors of Lumpy Bottom, Potters Crumpy and Winklebutty came together to seek a solution to the growing tensions.

The Earl of Lumpy Bottom suggested racing porcupines instead of goats. But it turned out that porcupines were very lazy and refused to race without the encouragement of a jockey or rider. After three somewhat unsuccessful racing trials, the jockeys of the region all went on strike, citing unacceptable working conditions.

The mayor of Potters Crumpy suggested a seafood Olympics. They would bring together the best and strongest crayfish, crabs, and lobsters of the region for a four-day oceanic extravaganza of elite sporting competition. Events would include wrestling, boxing, gymnastics, and weightlifting.

Competitors from across the region gathered in Potters Crumpy. Unfortunately, after a successful opening ceremony, on day two of the competition the athletes all inexplicably vanished. The reason for their absence is unclear to this day.

Some believe it was alien abductions; others believe a wormhole opened in space and time, triggered by government research. The ultimate truth remains a much-discussed mystery.

Inexplicably, sales of tartare sauce also rose tenfold during this period.

The case was officially solved years later by Lumpy Bottom's greatest private detective and crime author, Constable Peter Pavlova, the so-called Cheese Detective.

"It was them that done it ... probably," Pavlova had declared, in what would become his famous catchphrase, as he made the arrest of the century.

The then Sausage and Small Meat King of Potters Crumpy, Mario Mortadella, was arrested for the seafood abductions. He was ultimately found guilty and received fifteen years in the Potters Crumpy Penitentiary for the Impenitent. He asserted his innocence to the bitter end.

Not a single crustacean was ever recovered, and the only evidence linking Mario to the abductions was an anonymous tip-off from a source in Lumpy Bottom.

Conspiracy theorists remain unconvinced by the explanation.

Finally, the Duke of Winklebutty suggested whippet racing. Whippets were lean and fast, and no one would bother trying to eat them because they were so scrawny and hard to catch. They were even-tempered and quiet but had a good sense of humour deep down.

The jockeys of the district were suspicious at first. Most were still smarting from the porcupine debacle. It took some time, but they eventually adjusted to the new racing style.

Most jockeys grew to love racing whippets, which were fast, comfortable, and exciting to ride – the complete opposite of porcupines.

The biggest issue was that the whippets were much smarter than the jockeys and raced better without the unnecessary burden of a small, irritating person whipping them while they tried to win a race.

Several races were held without jockeys, until, in response to complaints from the public and bookmakers, the Whippet

Racing Board ruled that all whippets must be ridden by a jockey.

The racing public liked jockeys because it was more fun to watch crashes when jockeys were riding. The bookmakers preferred jockeys because they could be bribed to lose races, something whippets would never, ever do.

The inaugural race was held in Winklebutty and was originally called the Bum Bottoms Plains Cup. It was an immediate success. After that, for marketing and economic purposes, the race would be held in a different town each year.

Eventually, it was renamed the Winklebutty Cup, not after the town, but in memory of the Duke, who had died in an unfortunate cheese-eating incident a week before the big race.

This autumn, the cup would once more be held in Winklebutty. And it would not be just any race. It was the 113th Cup, which in whippet time was almost exactly 111 years. Whippets called this year's race the 'won-one one', and this year, on the 111th anniversary, whippets would come not just from the shire but from the entire region and beyond.

This Winklebutty Cup would be a once-in-a-lifetime event, an unmissable extravaganza of whippet equestrian excellence, and Destiny's one and only chance to save their home.

No wonder she was feeling a bit stressed.

CHAPTER 18

STUPID BUFFALO WHOM I HAVEN'T EATEN YET

Fate's Fur Art was, as fate would have it, a cheetah and not a whippet. But nor was he just any type of cheetah; he was a South American cheetah.

South American cheetahs are not quite as big or as fast as their African cousins, but they are twice as mean and not quite twice as stupid. Cheetahs are, after all, not renowned for their intelligence or good humour. In fact, there are no words in the cheetah language that mean 'funny' or 'joke', since cheetahs don't need to use those words unless describing the actions of non-cheetahs.

The cheetah phrase for a joke told by a non-cheetah is 'Grumple – grr ... err', which literally translates as, 'stupid non-cheetah whom I haven't eaten yet'. Cheetahs don't really have many friends.

Cheetahs can laugh, but usually only a sarcastic laugh that a cheetah might make when one of their friends falls over and gets trampled by a herd of rhinoceroses.

So far, there is only one documented joke ever made by a cheetah. It goes as follows.

Q: How many cheetahs does it take to change a light bulb?

A: Cheetahs don't change light bulbs. Call a buffalo. They

are stupid and will change it for you. Stupid buffalo whom I haven't eaten yet."

Fate's Fur Art was your typical South American cheetah, except even meaner and even more stupider.

In their natural South American habitat, cheetahs have only two enemies: tree monkeys and otters. Of course, as cheetahs are much faster than other land animals, they don't fear lions, elephants or even rhinos, which they can outrun with three paws tied behind their backs. Tree monkeys, however, have the advantage of height and camouflage.

Tree monkeys sneak up on cheetahs from high in the treetops and drop coconuts on them. Coconuts, however, are tasty and valuable, so monkeys rarely waste them. Instead, they happily throw their own poo at the unsuspecting big cats. Cheetahs hate this, which makes them both furious and smelly. Monkey dung sticks particularly firmly to cat fur, and there's not much the cheetahs can do about it, since they can't climb very well. (Well, actually, they can climb quite well, but they are very scared of heights, so they choose not to.) All they can do is curse the monkeys and move on.

As for the otters, well that's a different kettle of fish altogether. Otters despise cheetahs, who despise otters twice as much back. If a pack of otters surrounds a cheetah, they'll beat it mercilessly with their tails. Fate's Fur Art – or, as he was formerly known, Melville – had been on the receiving end of an otter beating when Chad Cheerio stumbled across him.

Chad had been on a scouting mission in the Lower Amazon Delta, looking for new and delicious animals to make shoes from, when he'd spotted the group of otters assaulting Melville. Using the discordant tones of his French horn, which he carried with him wherever he explored, Chad was able to scare off the otters.

Initially, his plan had been to make some premium racing boots and a spotty fur rug out of Melville. Quite by accident, however, he discovered that with a good coat of butter, some seasoning, and a dab of shoe polish, Melville resembled a large racing whippet!

After some experimentation with the formula, and with regular grooming, Chad entered Melville into his first whippet race: The Upper Boroughs Invitational. He changed the cat's name to Fate's Fur Art, and the rest, as they say, is history.

Fate's Fur Art became unbeatable throughout the whippet-racing circuit. He beat all the greats.

He dominated Wellington's Other Boot. He destroyed Madame Pomfrey's Plomp. And he humiliated Virginia's Angina. He beat all the whippets except one: Destiny's Poo.

Due to an array of scheduling issues and sponsorship conflicts, the two never met on the racetrack. Just as they were finally due to face off at the Potters Crumpy Seaside Invitational, Destiny's Poo suddenly, and unexpectedly, retired.

No one knew the full story behind her mysterious retirement. She was only seventeen years old, still in her prime in whippet-racing years. Angeli Cup was getting on a bit, but she had several years left in her before she handed the reins to a younger jockey.

Some speculated that Destiny was scared of losing to Fate's Fur Art. Others whispered about a complicated betting scandal involving a syndicate of porcupine criminals.

Only three people knew the whole truth of what had happened, and they weren't telling. Not a chance, never ever ...

or at least, not just yet. (Well, okay, you dragged it out of me! Destiny lost her sense of smell!)

CHAPTER 19

THERE CAN BE ONLY ONE

"Great session today, Destiny. I think we're almost ready to race," Sally-Dee whispered as she groomed Destiny's coat with Rex. It turned out that porcupine quills, while not great as toilet brushes, were perfect for whippet grooming.

"She looks mighty fast," said a voice from behind the stable door.

Sally-Dee looked up and lifted her eyebrows.

"I'm Chad, in case you were wondering," the voice continued. It was a calm, reassuring voice, much like how talcum powder might sound if it were a voice.

"I wasn't," another voice replied – a voice that was unmistakeably Sally-Dee's voice and sounded more like hot asphalt.

Chad sauntered into the stables. His voice followed a few seconds later. "You must be Sally-Dee. Sally-Dee Pickles. That's a bit of a mouthful. What should I call you?"

"You shouldn't ... er ... call me, that is."

"I like your spirit." Chad strode over to Destiny. "She looks strong. Great racing legs!" He slapped Destiny's hindquarters.

Destiny gave an unimpressed yelp of discouragement.

"She's a fine animal," Chad continued. "No wonder she's a favourite to run second."

At that, Destiny growled an irate whippet growl, which, to the untrained ear, sounded like a ripe lemon being squeezed. To the astute ear, however, it was clearly malicious and excessively hostile.

Even Rex was taken slightly aback by Destiny's aggression and by the unnecessary simile that risked triggering his lemoniphobia.

Chad remained completely unaware. "Nothing personal, Sally-Dee. I like you. There can, of course, be only one winner."

Chad was, of course, incorrect. In lemming steeplechasing, for instance, everyone who finishes is crowned a winner. Outsiders to the sport incorrectly assume that this ritual of awarding every finisher a gold medal is token symbolism that dilutes the sport's competitive nature, but nothing could be further from the truth. The rule was introduced primarily because no lemming *had* ever finished. The obstacle course was so difficult by its very nature that not only had no entrant completed it in its first seventy years, but nearly half the entrants who'd tried had either died or been permanently and severely injured.

The reasons for the race's difficulty were complicated and controversial. The inventor and sponsor of the first ever Lemming Steeplechase Eisteddfod was Duke Francis Autumnrump, a sportsman, philanthropist and hopeless gambler. Having lost the family fortune, he found himself on the bad side of a cartel of porcupine loan sharks.

He decided to hold a rigged sporting event and bet on the winner. To invite high levels of betting, he gave exceptional odds on the race. He collected thousands of shillings in bets, more than enough to cover his debts. The only problem was that he'd have to pay out the race winners, which would bankrupt him. So, he devised a loophole. If no lemming ever finished, Duke

Autumnrump would never have to pay out any money. Thusly, he used his engineering and gambling skills to make a lemming steeplechase racetrack so devilishly difficult, so deviously dangerous that no lemming could possibly hope to finish it.

For many years, the Lemming Steeplechase Eisteddfod flew in the face of the adage 'there can only be one' – because there were none, certainly no winners and fewer and fewer contenders.

Then, one year, an industrious lemming from the Lower Colon Counties, one Laurel Saint Gerbil, managed to crack the course and become the first ever finisher.

After that, it became common for multiple lemmings to complete the course. In honour of all the injured and deceased lemmings who'd tried, all finishers were crowned winners. Such a mockery did it make of the dictum 'there can only be one' that the phrase fell completely out of use in common vernacular. It was instead replaced with the saying, 'Not everyone wins, especially if they accidently die or break something.'

Chad seemed completely unaware of this important historical fact as he continued to chat to Sally-Dee.

"Nice saddle. What sort of leather is it?" He picked up Destiny's tiny saddle and held it in the palm of his hand.

"Not leather." Sally-Dee sneered. "It's bamboo and hemp. It helps absorb unpleasant saddle odours. You should get yourself one. I recommend the jumbo size, which is best for enormous arses like yourself."

Chad put the saddle down and ambled over to the stable door. "Well, it has been a pleasure. For you, more than me, but a pleasure, nonetheless. Good luck, Sally-Dee."

He left the stable.

His voice left at about the same time.

His smell lingered for a few minutes more before it, too, realised it was unwelcome and also left.

CHAPTER 20
STINKY CHEESE TUESDAY

It was the day that came four days before the race, an annual occasion historically known as 'Stinky Cheese Tuesday' despite it rarely falling on a Tuesday.

The event's exact origins were obscured in myth, uncertainty, and a certain amount of innuendo involving the names of cheeses that sounded slightly rude.

The most popular theory held that in the wake of the 23rd Winklebutty Cup, which was held in Lumpy Bottom that summer, the toe fungus plague returned. Stinky cheese was, at least for a number of years, thought to combat stinky toe. Eventually, after every resident in the Upper and Lower Colon Counties had been forced to ingest many pounds of stinky cheese, doctors accepted that perhaps there was no credible scientific evidence to support the theory.

Even with the benefit of hindsight, it's difficult to explain why anyone even *thought* that eating stinky cheese would affect the lethality of a fungal foot infection.

Albertonio Gorgonzola – one of the leading intellectuals at the time and, by an unrelated coincidence, the owner of Albertonio's Stinky Cheese Bazaar – was at the forefront of the public health campaign to fight stinky toe.

'If you don't eat stinky cheese, you are a murderous, cannibal baby-killer who should be locked away forever!' was the influential and catchy slogan of the Stinky Toe Health Campaign.

Mr Gorgonzola, who was not a qualified doctor, would later calculate that his stinky cheese campaign had saved thousands of lives – figures that were never confirmed by any statistical or scientific studies.

Mr Gorgonzola made more than ten million shillings from stinky cheese sales – figures that *were* confirmed by the tax office of Lower Lumpy Bottom, which is still chasing him for unpaid tax.

Albertonio's Stinky Cheese Bazaar remained the chief sponsor of the Winklebutty Cup for a further ten seasons, until a health scandal involving quite a lot of explosive diarrhoea caused the permanent closure of his enterprise.

In an unrelated coincidence, his bazaar unexpectedly exploded and burnt to the ground just before health inspectors were due to inspect it. Mr Gorgonzola – in an even less-related coincidence – collected a large sum of insurance money and promptly vanished.

His whereabouts remain unknown, although he is rumoured to be living on a private island off the coast of Weinercrump.

By an unusual but even more completely unrelated coincidence, Rocco Parmigiana quickly became the cup's primary cheese sponsor.

Each season, tradition required the presentation of a new official 'Cheese of the Cup'. One of Rocco's first and most successful cheeses was the Pepperoni Parmigiano, followed by the exclusive but delicate Gorgonzola Gateau.

Rocco Parmigiana took his stinky cheese duties very seriously.

Each racing season, on Stinky Cheese Tuesday, the official cheese of the Winklebutty Cup was revealed. Usually, the cheese presented would be a barometer of what the entire cheese world would be nibbling on that season.

The fromagarazzi would be abuzz with rumour and mystery in the weeks leading up to Stinky Cheese Tuesday. Every cheese afficionado had an opinion. *Cheese Connoisseur Monthly* proudly announced that this would be the year for the limburger cheese to rise to glory.

Cheese Weekly predicted a resurgence of gorgonzola.

'**COME ON HOME, CAMEMBERT**' was the headline of the *Winklebutty Tribune*, as it made its prediction.

The *Lumpy Bottom Examiner* favoured maasdam making a return. Everyone had an opinion. There was even betting on the outcome of the official cheese!

Only one person in the district knew for sure which cheese would be announced as the official cheese of the 113th Winklebutty Cup, and he was not telling. That person was, at that very moment, in his factory perfecting the recipe of his finest, most elaborate cheese creation.

He had been experimenting through the winter months, mixing and melding different flavours and concoctions to create a masterpiece – a truly cheesy legacy that generations would remember him by.

And so it was that at 3:35 am, Rocco Parmigiana stood in his large factory, and yelled. "I've done it! I have finally done it. Look at this! Can you see it?"

"Err, looks like cheese, Boss," Mr Humperdinck said.

"Cheese? *Cheese*, you imbecile! This is not just CHEESE. This is *the* cheese. This is the cheese of all cheeses, the greatest cheese in the history of cheesiness."

"Ha ha, ha ha. Err, ha ha!" Humperdinck laughed along,

having learned to chuckle at will whenever Mr Parmigiana did. "What sort of cheese is it?"

"This, my dear Humperdinck, is the ultimate and final evolution of cheese. This is a triple S – a Sausage Saint Subray."

"Err, so it's cheese with sausage meat in it?"

"No, Mr Humperdinck. Nothing could be further from the truth. The triple S is *not* a cheese with sausage in it – that would be derivative and unoriginal. This is something new, something completely different. This is a sausage with cheese in it! Ha ha ha, ha hah."

CHAPTER 21

AN 'ISTORICAL TREASURE

Almost exactly some time ago, Angeli Cup and Destiny had won their fifth Winklebutty Cup, which Angeli still remembered as if it were five minutes ago.

She remembered she and Destiny striding across the ceremonial goat-hair carpet as the crowd chanted a traditional whippet-racing victory song:

> *"You are the whippiest whippet,*
> *The best to ever race,*
> *Go, skinny whippet!*
> *Time to feed your face."*

Destiny had waved to the crowd, pumping her fists in the air and blowing kisses. She was naturally shy, but the occasion demanded a certain showmanship, so Destiny had done her best to appease the masses.

She was wearing a black cap from her major sponsor Fungaway, for whom she was contracted to promote Fungaway Toe Fungus Cream. 'Don't let toe fungus get in the way!' was their uninspiring slogan, which Destiny had to work into as many answers as possible in her post-race media interviews. She did not enjoy this aspect of her work, but no racing whippet did.

"You rode a great race," a young and not-yet-bald Phil Schiessenburger had announced.

Angeli Cup blushed sightly. She was younger then, but not any less of anything else, and she had never been one to take compliments.

Destiny had also blushed, which for a dog involves giving off a very subtle scent indicating humility. Unfortunately, Destiny made a slight error and instead gave off a scent indicating that she wished to fight any dog that looked at her to the death. Luckily, none of the humans noticed. The other racing whippets noticed, however, and were not impressed.

"It was Destiny who won. I was just along for the ride," insisted Angeli, who looked a little forlorn.

Maybe toe fungus is getting in the way of her life, thought Destiny, who was still trying to think of a way to reference her major sponsor.

The crowd roared as Destiny, Angeli, and Phil strolled through. The dogs in the crowd were especially rowdy.

"Who's that?" Angeli asked Phil, gesturing towards a rotund man who broke eye contact and lumbered into the throng.

"He works for the Cheese Lord," Phil replied, jerking his chin toward Rocco, the Sausage Baron of Lumpy Bottom. "But you should celebrate! You've got a winner's ceremony to attend."

Phil patted Angeli's shoulder as she and Destiny moved to the ceremonial podium. Angeli and Destiny climbed the rickety wooden stairs to the platform where the runners-up were already waiting.

Mrs Pumphrey's Undergarments had defied the bookmakers to come second, and Wellington's Other Boot had run a disappointing third. Also on the pedestal stood a marble whippet. On its nose rested a porcelain plate, and on the plate lay the ceremonial cheese – a truffle casu marzu.

As tradition required, Destiny took a long bow. News photographers scrambled to get the best shot of the victorious whippet. Reporters jostled to interview the winner and her jockey, yelling questions from behind the security fence.

Angeli Cup still had butterflies in her tummy. In minutes, she would be receiving the victory casu marzu. Usually, Angeli's anxieties settled after the race, but this time, they remained.

For as long as people and dogs could remember, tradition dictated that the winning jockey take the first and largest bite of the cheese before offering their racing whippet a small portion of what remained. It was a tradition Angeli Cup despised. For several years, she had been a vocal critic of this ritual, which she was sure represented whippet inequality and repression.

Seeing the whippet, and indeed all animals, as her equal, she wanted to share her cheese equally with Destiny. Angeli was also lactose-intolerant, so eating cheese usually made her break out in hives.

She had lobbied the Whippet Racing Board to change the rule. The rule, however, had been inscribed many years ago on a strip of leathered goat colon that the First Earl of Winklebutt had somehow extracted from an angry mountain goat while it was still alive. (Please don't ask any more details about this incident, as it is a rather distasteful and messy story.)

However, as the parchment was *an 'istorical treasure*, it simply could not be changed. It was carefully kept at the Winklebutty Bigbooty Museum and Burlesque Cabaret Restaurant – a complicated merger that had secured the financial survival of both businesses.

Lord Fartmaster the Twelfth was the visionary who had combined a struggling museum and an on-its-knees cabaret show into a successful entertainment extravaganza.

'History by day, cover story by night,' was the slogan that had made the place famous. Stored here, for all the county to see, were the poorly spelt but still legible scrawlings of Earl Winklebutt the First. Engraved on the strip of partially rotting intestine were the following words:

The victa will ~~fast~~ feats on the cheese and his ~~dog~~ steed will have thre crumbes.

The Whippet Racing Board had not the slightest idea what it meant, and perhaps nor did the Earl, as it was reasonably well documented that he often consumed enough of the town's hallucinogenic mushrooms to sedate a pod of minke whales. Nor did they especially care what any jockey did with their victory cheese, as long as they did not attack any members of the Board with it. But Angeli Cup interpreted this decree very literally.

To her, it meant the winning jockey should eat most of the cheese and give the dog just three crumbs. She followed these rules dutifully, as she followed all rules.

After every race they had won, despite her lactose intolerance and her toe fungus, Angeli had eaten her victory cheese and given Destiny a mere three crumbs. Angeli then usually broke out in a severe rash and spent two days on the toilet.

"Look, you can take the cheese home, paint it lilac, and raise it as your grandson for all I care," the head of the Board had boomed at Angeli on the several occasions she'd complained. "But we can't change the parchment. It is an 'istorical treasure! Besides which, we have no idea how to open this glass case!" He tapped it with his cane dramatically. "And Bernie the caretaker thinks the smell of ancient fermented goat guts could be lethal."

Unfortunately, it had never been in Angeli Cup's nature to

break the rules. She was a stickler for the law. She never crossed the road on a red light. She never drove fast, and she never talked in the quiet section of the library. She followed rules that didn't even exist yet, just to be sure she didn't break any rules that might be written in the future.

"What if they change the law and that becomes illegal?" Angeli would ask whenever anyone suggested doing something ground-breaking, such as making an omelette with foreign ingredients.

The injustice of it made her angry and tore up her insides, like it had the mountain goat former owner of the parchment.

She loved Destiny. Destiny wasn't just a dog to her – she was her best friend, her equal. Angeli Cup didn't care about the colour of her fur or the number of legs she had! To her, Destiny wasn't a whippet, she was ... well, she was Destiny's Poo!

It was in the midst of this emotional turmoil that Angeli Cup made a fateful decision – a decision that was to affect her and Destiny's lives for ever more.

Having won the Winklebutty Cup, and being filled with self-righteous anger, Angeli Cup ignored all her instincts and did the unthinkable. She broke the rules!

After Destiny proudly leapt onto the podium, Angeli took the victory cheese in her shaking hands. The crowd cheered wildly, although all the dogs remained snarly and on edge. Angeli took a nibble of the cheese. She knew what she was going to do. Breaking off the larger portion of the casu marzu, she offered it to her victorious steed.

"This is for you, my friend. You deserve it."

Destiny smiled and raised her back left leg in a sign of canine love and respect." Then she took the cheese in both front paws and ate it.

No one in the crowd took any notice of this small but very significant act of rebellion. They continued to cheer, and the dogs continued to growl. Phil Schiessenburger alone knew the magnitude of what had just happened. His eyes widened, and he shook his head.

Meanwhile, Destiny gazed up at Angeli with a mixture of admiration and disgust. Her admiration was for Angeli's uncompromising values and support for dog equality. Her disgust was that Angeli had handed her three-quarters of the victory casu marzu that wriggled with live maggots. As Angeli fed her the cheese, Destiny could see the tiny larvae squirming about inside. It was about as inviting as elephant vomit, which, of course, some dogs think is a delicacy, but not Destiny, who you'll remember was funny about smells.

Yet, Destiny loved Angeli. Overcoming all her natural gag reflexes and urges to spew, she swallowed the victory cheese. Immediately, Destiny went slightly red and then fainted.

The crowd thought it was shock or excitement, but that was the last memory Destiny could remember until she woke up in the hospital three hours later.

CHAPTER 22

DESTINY'S SPEW

"How is she going this morning?" Angeli asked the doctor.

After Destiny's collapse, Phil had immediately rushed Angeli and Destiny to the Potters Crumpy Hospital for Crustaceans, Porcupines and Furry Creatures, where Destiny had been kept in overnight while she continued to produce some impressive technicolour yawns.

When she awoke, the unthinkable news was delivered.

"She's fine. Good as gold. Fit as a fiddle. Darndest thing, though, she now can't smell a thing," replied the doctor. "That should not be a major issue, however. Unless she's a racing dog, in which case she's pretty much stuffed. No whippet can race if she can't smell."

When officials later examined what was left of the victory casu marzu, it was found to have been contaminated with a Lumpy Bottom lava pepper, the smallest and hottest of all chillis. In an instant, it had fried Destiny's nose receptors.

Without her sense of smell, Destiny could no longer detect the faintest whiff of victory – or anything else. It was a symptom you didn't know you had until you had it, and once you got it, you then knew you had it – Chronic Obstructive Volcano

Intestinal Disease, or at least that's what the official scare campaign for Lumpy Bottom lava chilli poisoning had to say about the matter. Its catchy slogan was 'You smell – not!'

Whippets need their sense of smell to race, as it gives them the passion and urge to win. Without smell, Destiny could still run, but she may never again have the urge to cross the finish line.

Surprisingly, Destiny was fine with that. She was already the only five-time winner of the most prestigious whippet race in the world. She had nothing left to prove. And now she would never have to smell another dog's butt ever again.

Angeli Cup, however, was never the same. A tear dripped down her left cheek, and her lips quivered ever so slightly. The jockey would never stop blaming herself for having given Destiny the first bite of the cheese. "Thank you for your care, Dr Putz," she muttered.

Angeli put her hand on Destiny's paw. "Rest up and you'll be back racing in no time, Destiny," she lied – and she knew it.

So did Destiny.

Both of them knew that they would never race again, ever.

Until now, that is.

(Well ... actually, neither of them knew that bit at the time either, which they now know, and so do you. But at the time, they did not know, and both knew she would never race again, you know? It's complicated!)

CHAPTER 23

NO STRINGS ATTACHED

The week before their last-ditch attempt to win the Winklebutty Cup, Angeli decided to visit Phil at the bank.

She was worried. If Destiny didn't win, they could all lose everything.

"Angeli, I would love to give you more money. You're family, after all. But I can't. The bosses won't let me. You owe two thousand shillings, and unless you get that money by the end of the month, the bank will sell The Last Lap – probably to you-know-who."

Seeing Angeli's crestfallen face, he added, "Look, I will try to help you. I will try to stall the purchase. But no one must know. If Rocco finds out I'm helping you, he'll put me in the meat grinder along with the chihuahuas. No one must know I've given you any money." He chuckled nervously. "All I have is enough to cover your next interest payment. That might buy you a little time. But if the bank audits your account, I'm done for, so don't tell a soul."

"I appreciate you putting your neck on the line for me." Angeli gave him a brief hug. "I've no one else to lean on."

"Deposit this into your account tomorrow." He passed her a

bank cheque for 500 shillings. "If the teller asks, say it was an inheritance. Sign here to accept the cheque." He pointed to a dotted line and handed Angeli a ballpoint pen.

"How can I ever repay you?"

"No strings attached, cousin. But, if you insist, you know the way to my heart. Bring me a few of those truffle mushrooms. You know how much I love them."

"Sure. There are so many the dogs can't eat them all anyway." Angeli gave him another hug, this time slightly longer. "I'd better get back to The Last Lap before anyone notices I'm missing."

CHAPTER 24
BREAK A LEG

The day before the Winklebutty Cup never had any special significance, nor did it have a fancy name. This summer, it fell on a Wednesday. To Angeli Cup, it felt much like another day.

She did not generally get nervous before races. Her routine was much the same as any other day.

Sally-Dee, however, was more stressed than she had been since primary school. It was her last chance to get some practise.

As Sally-Dee and Destiny galloped around the track, in the distance a small bald man stared at them through large binoculars. Next to him stood a larger man. The first man looked a bit like Rocco Parmigiana, while the other man ... well, I really couldn't say – it truly was a very long distance away.

Meanwhile, out on the racetrack, Destiny slowly increased her speed.

"Go, Destiny! You're doing excellent!" Sally-Dee whispered. "Am I doing, okay? I hope I'm not riding wrong. Oh ... I knew it. I'm riding badly, and it's slowing you down. I'm such a bad rider. You deserve better."

Destiny was not listening. She was quite used to ignoring Sally-Dee's self-sabotage, so it was easy to block it out and focus on racing. Instead, she made supportive grunts at regular intervals, which usually appeased Sally-Dee, but not today.

"Oh, you're just saying that, Destiny! I know you're lying. I'm an awful jockey, and everyone knows it. How could I ever live up to Angeli 'Golden' Cuppppppppp–aarrrrrggghhhhhh!"

Destiny kept on racing faster than ever while making supportive grunts. She was in the zone. She had already crossed the finish line and was looking up at the stopwatch that hung next to the racetrack, which showed a time of 3 minutes flat – a personal best. If Destiny could run that fast on race day, she was a real chance to win.

Feeling happy and excited, the whippet looked up to congratulate Sally-Dee. But on the saddle, where Sally-Dee was meant to be, was nothing but empty space.

Unusual, thought Destiny, although it did explain why she had run so rapidly.

Destiny scouted the racetrack and soon made out the unmistakable figure of Sally-Dee.

She was lying on the ground and trying to breakdance while yodelling loudly.

An odd thing to do, thought Destiny, but it was not her business to question Sally-Dee's creative outlets. She ran back over to where Sally-Dee was vibing.

"I think I've broken my leg," Sally-Dee moaned. Her right leg was twisted in a very unusual way, the shin bone visibly poking through her skin.

Given this new information, Sally-Dee's behaviour seemed to make more sense. On reflection, Destiny realised that Sally-Dee wasn't trying to yodel – she was screaming in pain. She figured it probably related to the jockey's broken leg, although Destiny was not a fully qualified orthopaedic surgeon – having dropped out of medical studies in her second year to follow her racing dreams – and she could not rule out other causes of excruciating pain, such as severe indigestion, gout, or gallstones.

Destiny was also still uncertain why Sally-Dee was breakdancing on the racetrack, which seemed a peculiar thing to do given the compound fracture of her leg. Then again, Destiny was not a qualified DJ.

Sally-Dee was not a qualified disc jockey either. She was not even a qualified whippet jockey, which was probably how she had found herself in this situation. Destiny was, however, an accepting and open-minded dog. If Sally-Dee wanted to breakdance right after snapping her shinbone, well, it was entirely her choice.

Eventually, the dancing subsided, and Angeli arrived to drive Sally-Dee to hospital, which seemed a better option than driving her to a dance class, or to distraction. Sally-Dee seemed to agree, although it was difficult to be sure of that, since she continued to yodel all the way to hospital.

CHAPTER 25
THE HYPOCRITICAL OATH

"Thank you for seeing Sally-Dee so quickly, Dr Putz."

"Quickly? Are you certain? I thought you'd been waiting since yesterday."

"Oh no, it has only been a few minutes. We are ever so grateful," Angeli said.

"Oops. Oh, my mistake. I must have grabbed the wrong chart. You won't tell anyone, will you?"

"Tell them what?"

"That I saw you quickly. It's against hospital policy, and I think it also breaks the Hypocritical Oath. We're meant to keep you waiting for much, much longer."

"How long?"

"Well ... until you leave."

Angeli shrugged in confusion. "But how does that help the patient?"

"Help the patient? Ha, ha, HA! You make me laugh. That's a good one. You're joking, aren't you?"

Angeli Cup was not joking.

"Well, I can tell you a joke, if you'd like," suggested Dr Putz. "How many doctors does it take to change a lightbulb?"

"I'd prefer an update on Sally-Dee. Is her leg any better? Will she be discharged today? Will she still be able to race tomorrow?"

"Yes, yes, no, and three," Dr Putz replied.

"What do you mean?"

"Sally-Dee is better. She can go home tomorrow. She won't be able to race tomorrow. And it takes three doctors to change a lightbulb."

"That's awful news. Are you sure?"

"Yes! It usually takes at least three. Let me explain, it takes one doctor to—

"Please don't. Are you sure she won't be able to race?"

"Well, yes, of course, I'm sure. Her shinbone is shattered. She would have to be some sort of superhuman whippet-racing machine to be able to compete in this condition, which, it appears, she is clearly not."

Dr Putz added in a not-very-quiet-at-all whisper, "Besides, Destiny came in earlier, and she asked me to not clear Sally-Dee to race tomorrow. She thinks Sally-Dee is a menace on the racetrack and should only be riding emotionally blunted lemmings. She also specifically asked me to not tell anyone about our discussion, especially not ... you."

"Er, so why are you telling me?" Angeli put her hands on her hips.

"My bad! I'm a blabbermouth. Can't keep a secret to save my life."

"Aren't you meant to keep patient information confidential?"

"Not sure. Ethics was never my strong subject at medical school. I'll take your word for it, though. You seem like the type who would know that sort of stuff and follow the rules."

"I hope you're better at fixing people than maintaining confidentiality."

"No, not really. I am the official race doctor, though. I'm great with racing injuries – not really at treating them, but certainly at photographing them. I've got a collection of gruesome racing injury photos. Perhaps I could show them to you sometime."

A loudish knocking interrupted them. A few seconds later, the door swung open, and two people walked into the room.

It seems reasonable to assume first that they were people and second that one of those people was responsible for the knocking, although, admittedly, an astute reader such as yourself would never jump to premature conclusions.

"Well, well, well, well, if it isn't the jockey herself. Seems like you've had an injury, haven't you?" The words seemed to be escaping from the mouth of a mid-size female wearing a police officer's uniform. Next to her was a slightly taller, male-looking person who was also wearing a police officer's uniform, although it was still not totally clear exactly who this pair were or what they did for a living.

"I'm Constable Olivia Oregano, and this is my partner, Sergeant Paul Pavlova. We are police officers." Their statement seemed to have clarified a number of hitherto unclear issues.

"Well, lucky you explained. I thought you might have been adult entertainers," Dr Putz replied.

"Trying to be clever are you, Dr Putz?" Olivia said in what appeared to be a stern, aggressive tone but was actually an attempt to be gentle and friendly, which her therapist had recommended she try to help ease her anger issues.

"No, not at all, Constable Oregano. It's just that Dr Phillips is having a buck's party on G floor. I thought you might have just gotten lost. He throws some great parties. You should come to one of his shindigs. They're legendary. Last year, for instance, he had the Moscow Dance Troupe perform an ABBA tribute show. It was to die for."

"I'm not going to his stupid buck's party. I would sooner choke on my own vomit." Olivia turned to face Sally-Dee in the hospital bed. "Er ... let me rephrase that. I would prefer not to attend the party, which I'm sure Dr Putz would enjoy, but which

I do not believe I would enjoy as much. Now, if I may continue." Olivia took a small breath and continued, "Sally-Dee Pickles, we have come to inform you that—"

She was interrupted by a loud *thump* on the door, followed by a brief scream. Phil and Destiny staggered in. Phil was wearing a green party hat and holding his wrist to his forehead. Destiny was inexplicably covered in glitter.

"Where did that door come from ...?" *Hiccup.* "That is a really stupid place for a door! Ohh, hello Village People. How did you get here so quickly ...?" *Hiccup*. Phil stumbled towards Pavlova and started to move his arms in a vague, wafting Y movement. "You may need to arrest me, Officer Beefcake."

He lurched sideways and crooked his arms into what appeared to be an M-shape above his head. He shook both wrists at the person who identified as a police officer, or maybe he was trying to make a C. It was very hard to tell, given his level of incoordination. "I have been bad," he confessed.

"At dancing!" Angeli muttered under her breath.

Paul Pavlova pushed Phil's wrists away. "My name is *Sergeant* Pavlova." He pointed to his badge. "You are not, at this time, under arrest."

"But are you *sure,* Orrificer Beefy?" Phil winked.

"My name is not Officer Beefy!"

Phil narrowed his eyes suspiciously. "Now that you mention it, you have lost your muscles." *Hiccup.*

"You're incapacitated, aren't you?"

"That is a rather complicarated querestion." *Hiccup*. "For instance, define incapacitatitated."

Dr Putz pointed at Sally-Dee, whose leg was in a sling. "Her."

"It wasn't a question," Constable Oregano interrupted. "We have come to inform Ms Pickles that it appears her saddle was deliberately tampered with. I'm afraid she has been the victim of attempted foul play. Do any of you know anyone who might wish Ms Pickles to be injured so she could not race?"

A calm silence fell over the room.

Dr Putz, Angeli Cup and Sally-Dee were deep in thought, trying to figure out who might sabotage Sal's saddle.

Destiny had fallen asleep on the chair.

And Phil had already snuck back to floor G to dance with Officer Beefcake.

CHAPTER 26
THE WHIFF OF VICTORY

Sally-Dee was reclining in the lounge chair with her leg up, snoring loudly. A full-length plaster cast encased her left leg. All the whippets and porcupine residents of The Last Lap had signed it, leaving (mostly) supportive messages on it, except for Bugsy Pratwaffle, the cantankerous elderly porcupine resident from room 283.

He was a retired tattoo artist, most well-known for his hyper-realistic pirate tattoos as well as his atrocious spelling. "Owful ridding, don't quiet your day job," he had stabbed into the cast with his one remaining quill.

On a side note, Bugsy had been forced into hiding at The Last Lap after misspelling a girl's name on a man's tattoo. Turns out there is a world of difference between the names Jane and John, especially when the words 'Love You Forever' are permanently tattooed in front of it in large letters across someone's back.

Rex, in contrast, had drawn a rather rude picture on Sally-Dee's cast. In his defence, he insisted it was an Ancient Greek symbol representing health, hope and healing. This, he claimed, was the Spartan Infinity Mark – represented by a straight banana with two chicken eggs at its base.

Phil had written the customary but boring words 'Get better soon'– and he meant it. He was, however, not visiting The Last Lap to talk to Sally-Dee.

"I'll have to race. There is no other option." Angeli sighed as she sat down alongside Destiny and Rex at the oak table.

"You know that's not possible, Angeli. You are in no shape to race," Phil insisted. "And Rex, stop drawing rude symbols on Sally-Dee's cast!"

"Well, who else is there? I mean, Destiny can't race without a jockey. The rules are clear about that."

"Angeli, you have to be realistic. You can't race and neither can Sally-Dee."

"Who? What? Huh?" Sally-Dee woke up, rubbing her eyes.

"Face it. It's over," Phil continued. "You may have to accept that you'll have to sell The Last Lap."

"There is no way I would let Rocco take over this place!" Angeli stamped her foot and winced a little at the force of it.

"I know how you feel, cousin, but unless you want the porcupine to ride her, there's no way we can find a jockey in time."

Destiny stood up and wagged her tail. Rex wiggled his upper spines.

"Are you sure?" Sally-Dee interrupted.

"Sure, of what?" asked Phil, rubbing his chin.

"Rex thinks he can jockey Destiny. And Destiny thinks it's a great idea." Sally-Dee pointed at the two, who were both blushing with excitement.

"But what about Destiny's, well ... you know ... her little *issue*. Expecting her to win even though she has lost her ... well, you know what she has lost. I mean, she's a dog, after all. How can she possibly race if she has lost her smell?"

For a minute or two, no one spoke.

"What do you mean she can't smell?" Sally-Dee said.

"What do you mean *what do I mean*? It seems reasonably self-explanatory. Destiny cannot smell."

Another bout of silence was interrupted by a soft, gurgled whistling. It was the dulcet tone of a whippet passing wind. The fart's owner was Destiny, who had been on a low-carbohydrate, high-sauerkraut and seaweed diet for four weeks. The fart's stench was simultaneously indescribable and revolting.

"Oh, Dear God! That is appalling!" Phil muttered right before he fainted. As he fell, he struck his head on the wooden table, gifting him with peaceful, fragrance-free unconsciousness – a blissful state he would enjoy for a full twenty-eight seconds until the concussion lifted and he regained his faculties.

Schiessenburger began to cough and then to lightly convulse. He also become very aware of the imprecision of the English language to describe specific situations such as this.

"Well, maybe it isn't that self-explanatory after all," Angeli interrupted. "Let me explain. Destiny lost her ability to *detect* smells in a racing accident. However, her ability to *create* smells remains. It is safe to say that her ability to produce foetid, repugnant, vomit-inducing odours is better than it has ever been." She waved a hand in front of her face. "Her ability, however, to sniff odours has been severely depleted. In short, she can both smell and not smell at the same time. I hope that is clear."

The room went quiet again for a short period while the abomination continued to linger.

Whippets, it should be said, are smarter and more sophisticated than their oversized cousins, the greyhounds. Greyhounds can be encouraged to run by chasing pretend electric bunnies around a track; this is because scientific studies have shown that bigger dogs are always stupider than smaller dogs.

Whippets are far too intelligent to fall for the simplistic ruse of a pretend rabbit. Whippets run because they get a whiff of victory – not metaphorical victory, but literal victory. Winning for a whippet is accompanied by an intoxicating smell emitted by their own scent glands. Legendary racer and Last Lap resident Ethyl Winklepimple once described the fragrance as, 'an overwhelming and irresistible combination of squirrel vomit, mouldy cheese and well-aged buffalo dung'.

You probably have to be a whippet, or at least some sort of canine, to understand how truly addictive that smell can be.

In any case, this pheromone gave racing dogs the motivation to push themselves to the limits of dog endurance in the quest for racing glory. Without this motivation, no whippet could succeed. So, of course, everyone wondered how Destiny could possibly win the Winklebutty Cup when she had lost her olfactory senses.

Sally-Dee sat up and fluffed her cushions. "Maybe it's all a conspiracy. Maybe Destiny doesn't actually *need* to smell to race."

"Oh, Destiny definitely smells," Phil muttered, pinching his nose and sniffing.

"Maybe she is more than just a dog with an addiction to bad smells," Sally-Dee went on. "Maybe she's a person, a living, breathing, thinking person who can use her brain to race. She doesn't need scent to motivate her! She knows how important this race is! She knows that everything she cares for and everything she loves is on the line. *That* is far greater motivation that any smell."

Destiny stood up, stretched, and glanced at the people around her. Angeli Cup, Sally-Dee, Rex, and the rest of the residents of The Last Lap (even Bugsby Pratwaffle) were her family. They needed her, and she needed them.

She knew she would race, not for the smell, not for the glory, but for her family.

Sally-Dee was right: *that* was the only motivation Destiny needed.

CHAPTER 27
DEFINE LEGAL

One day before the Cup

It was the day before the Winklebutty Cup, and an emergency meeting of the National Whippet Racing Tribunal had been called.

In the long history of whippet racing, this had occurred on no more than three occasions – four if you counted the current meeting. Usually, it was for the purposes of arranging a last-minute replacement for jockeys who had been injured at the pre-race Winklebutty Cup Party. This year, like most years, the party was rather forgettable, primarily because no one who attended could recall much of anything after midnight.

The tribunal consisted of all the most important and senior members of the Whippet Racing Board who were well enough to attend on the morning after the pre-race Winklebutty Cup Party, and the tribunal members usually sent their respects to any injured riders and agreed to their replacements. This time, that happened to be just one person: Baron Blitz Von Crapper.

Angeli, Sally-Dee, Rex and Destiny were representing themselves, which did not appear to be going well.

"So, let me get this straight, Ms Cup," Von Crapper

questioned. "You can't ride the dog because you are too old and decrepit, so you wanted Ms Pickles to ride, but now Ms Pickles has broken her leg, and you want the porcupine to ride in her place. Is that correct?"

"Well, yes and no. I'm not too *old* to ride. I'm just not ... well ... let's say I'm just too experienced, if you know what I mean." Angeli winked her left eye and tilted her head briefly.

"No, not really. Besides, Ms Cup, you know the rules. They say an injured jockey can be replaced if – let me quote directly from the official racing almanac – '*If they are too inebriated or if they must leave the county at short notice to avoid being arrested*'. Never, however, in the long and honoured history of the Winklebutty Cup has the replacement jockey been a *porcupine*." He frowned over his spectacles at Rex.

"What's wrong with porcupines?" Sally-Dee bristled.

"Well, nothing, unless you happen to mistake one for a cushion. Let me tell you, young lady, that's not a mistake you want to make twice, is it?" he grumbled, rubbing his bottom. "So, I'm afraid I'm going to have to—"

"—approve your request and grant you permission to let that spiky weasel race," interrupted a voice very different to Baron Von Crapper's.

"Er, no. That's not what I was going to say. Who are you?" The original voice continued.

"No need to stand. I'm the one, the only, the legendary Ace – Ace Kermit McBalls, known to my friends as Ace McBalls and to my enemies as Ace McBalls," the voice continued. "Turns out my enemies are not that imaginative. But I digress. The issue is one of natural justice, which, Baron Von Crapper, can only be served by letting the weasel race." Ace slammed his open palm on the table, unfortunately striking a small tub of all-natural goats' milk yoghurt. Until this time, the yoghurt had gone unnoticed to everyone in the courtroom, and the contents had been unknown. (They turned out to be goats' milk yoghurt, which, with the power of hindsight and reading comprehension, makes complete sense). Now, freeing themselves from the limited confines of the tub, they had – much like their distant ancestor Leaping Lorelle – expanded their reach and leapt to distant areas of the room.

A slight pause was followed by a long snoring sound. Von Crapper lay on the bench with his eyes closed and a large dollop of yoghurt on his forehead.

"That was my lunch," Angeli Cup told Ace, gesturing to the tub.

"I think he's out." Ace ignored her and began shaking Von Crapper violently. "He really is unconscious."

"Should we call an ambulance or something?" Sally-Dee piped up.

"We should call for pizza. Meanwhile, how about I fill in the appeals form for Von Crapper?" Ace began writing out the paperwork.

"Are you sure that's legal?" Angeli peered over his shoulder.

"Of course it's legal! I would never break the law. I am a student lawyer *and* a self-help guru. Besides, what's illegal about ordering pizza?"

"Not the pizza! I mean filling out the forms for Von Crapper while he is passed out."

"Ohh ... that little thing. Well, define *legal*."

CHAPTER 28
RACE DAY

It was the 31st of September, the traditional date for the Winklebutty Cup. An electric energy enlivened Winklebutty and the surrounding boroughs. This was the day, the one and only day of the year, when everything else ground to a halt, and all eyes, ears, and noses were firmly focused on Butterscotchbottom Racecourse, the spiritual home of whippet racing.

In Potters Crumpy, the donut factories closed their doors and stopped donutting. The shops pulled down their shutters. Even the schools closed their classrooms, which did not matter much, since the children of Potters Crumpy were so notoriously stupid that a day off was not going to make the slightest difference to their already woeful academic performances.

In Lumpy Bottom, the gaming houses stopped play for the afternoon. Betting continued, but it was mostly done by telegram or carrier pigeon for the rest of the day. Pigeons never rested, even on this special day, although their delivery fees increased considerably.

From banks to pawn brokers, everything closed down. Even the sausage factory was supposed to stop sausaging and the delivery trucks to halt for one day only. It was, after all, the race that stopped people doing more important stuff until tomorrow.

In fact, unbeknownst to the people of Lumpy Bottom, the only thing still working was the Meat Emporium. The smoke that usually billowed from the sausage factory's chimney was being recycled, so as not to arouse suspicion. Inside, the *clink* and *clank* of the factory continued, Cup or no Cup.

At the racing stalls, Rex and Destiny paced anxiously. In two hours, they would be running the race of their lives. They knew how much was riding on this day. Everything.

Back at the factory, Rocco Parmigiana was perfecting this season's batch of sausages – bratwurst and meaty cheeses. He also knew how much was riding on this year's Winklebutty Cup.

Everything.

CHAPTER 29
A BIT OF "PEM"

"She looks good. Don't you think?"

"Good, yes. But not great."

"Oh, Phillip! Don't be such a half-a-glass-of-milk person."

"I think you mean glass half empty."

"Er, no. Why would you empty my glass?"

"All I'm saying, cousin, is that you have a lot riding on this race. And when I say a lot, I mean *everything*. And not just for you. Think of all the residents at The Last Lap. If Destiny doesn't win, everyone loses."

"I have faith in Destiny."

"I do, too. But wouldn't it be good if we had a ... well ... insurance policy to make sure Destiny is running at her best." Phil winked his left eye and tilted his head slightly. "If you *know what I mean*."

"Do you mean you have some sort of twitch? You might want to ask Dr Putz to look at that."

"No! I don't mean a twitch. I mean maybe we could help Destiny run a bit faster with a bit of pep. Or a little help from a 'pem' friend, if you *know what I mean*?"

"You're twitching again. What sort of help are you talking about?"

"Oh, for goodness' sake, Angeli. Do I have to spell it out? P.E.M. Don't be such a prude. This is professional racing. All the dogs are doing it." He lowered his voice to a whisper. "Why don't we give Destiny some dogtosterone?" Phil pulled his hand from his trouser pocket and placed a large yellow-and-green mushroom on the table.

Angeli, Destiny and Sally-Dee all made an 'ooh' type of sound. Rex farted, which was also an 'ooooohhhhh' type of sound, with a smell attached for dramatic effect.

"That's cheating!" Angeli announced.

"This is the real world, Angeli. You know how much is riding on this race? Anyway, think about it. How much do you really want to save The Last Lap?" Phil grabbed his hat and marched out the door.

Throughout their racing career, Destiny and Angeli Cup had never ever cheated or broken the rules. Except that one time at the Potters Crumpy Invitational when Angeli had inadvertently broken the dress code. (In her defence, both she and Destiny are colour blind, and to this day, Angeli feels shamefully guilty about wearing green pants instead of the required navy blue.)

Taking a performance enhancer, however, was a completely different level of cheating to wearing the wrong-coloured jodhpurs.

Dogtosterone was a performance enhancing mushroom (PEM) most commonly used by porcupine boxers and body builders to increase the strength and spikiness of their spines.

It was not the only PEM, but it was the most well-known, as its use had been popularised by musicians such as Warm Tea and Snoop Kitty. For a short time, the self-help guru Ace

McBalls had even promoted it as a path to spiritual enlightenment and self-actualisation.

Despite its benefits, dogtosterone was found to have unwanted side effects, including anger, hair loss, and scaly red skin blistering. Eventually, it was banned by every sporting organisation in the Lower Colon Counties, except the Lobster and Crustacean Martial Arts Association (LCMAA).

Its only medicinal use was for the treatment of third-degree toxic toe fungus, which, by an unrelated coincidence, almost all the racing whippets of the region always contracted in the weeks leading up to the Winklebutty Cup.

Destiny had been offered dogtosterone many times, but she had always refused. She told people that was because she had a rare fear of spotted mushrooms, known as champignonophobia. But the real reason she refused to take PEMs – the one she would never admit to anyone – was that her confidence often bordered on arrogance, so she didn't need even need it.

In her mind, Destiny was the best racing whippet of all time. In front of the cameras and media, she was a shy, self-deprecating champion. After every win, she would state how relieved she was to have crossed the line first and how close the race had been. She would talk up her adversaries, express how grateful she was for the prize money, and insist that she would probably lose the next race – but it was all just an act.

She knew she was the best.

She knew no one could get near her.

Sometimes, she would even slow down during her races, just to make the race more exciting. Often, she deliberately let herself get overtaken, just so she could come from behind at the last moment. In truth, she was completely arrogant.

Whenever Destiny trotted onto a racetrack, she did not just *think* she would win; she *knew* she would. She was the best whippet by a country mile, and probably by a city mile too. No one was ever quite sure how the two differed in length, since city miles were measured in French poodle poos per square metre and country miles were measured in dingo droppings per cubic hectare, so the mathematical conversion was beyond most in the boroughs, with the possible exception of Rex.

Regardless, Destiny was so powerful a racer that it would never, ever occur to her to take PEMs, because it never, ever occurred to her that anyone could even come close to beating her.

If the other dogs took dogtosterone, it only meant they might get a bit closer to her, so she'd cool her jets for a while to make it look like a close race.

Destiny had never lost a race that counted, but then again, she'd never had anything to lose either. Never, ever had she considered taking dogtosterone – until now.

She ambled over to the table and sniffed at the yellow-and-green mushroom a few times. She looked somewhat sheepishly at Angeli, who said nothing. There was nothing to say. It had never occurred to her that she, Destiny's Poo, could lose. But today?

Well, today was different.

Today, Destiny was older, weaker, and slower than she had ever been. She also had a terrible case of third-degree toxic toe fungus – of course.

Raising one paw, Destiny grabbed the mushroom, slipped it into her satchel and set off out the door for the racing stables.

Angeli still said nothing. There was still nothing to say ... at least for a few seconds until the stench of Rex's fart arrived.

"REX! For goodness' sake!"

CHAPTER 30
FURIOUS DURIANS

The 113th WBC began as it traditionally always did – with the tossing of the gherkin.

As the riders and their whippets lined up behind the starting line, Phil Schiessenburger clutched the pickle. When the gong rang, he would yeet it high into the air. When it hit the ground, the race would begin, just as it had for centuries – except for that one time when the pickle had been replaced by an aubergine, and another time when zucchini had been a last-minute stand-in. Neither vegetable had ever been as popular or as successful for tossing as the gherkin.

Initially, the WBC organisers had planned to toss a rotating roster of vegetables, fruits and legumes, highlighting the stable crops of the many boroughs that made up the region. That plan had been permanently scuppered by the unfortunate debacle of the 18th or 19th Cup (no one alive now could quite remember which).

What they did remember was that, in tribute to one of the poorest villages of the Lower Colon Counties, a down-on-its-luck place called Baggy End, the durian fruit had been chosen to start the race.

Durian is renowned for its tasty but unforgettably smelly

flesh. Humans, on the one hand, find the fruit's smell, which is something like a blend of off parmesan cheese blended with fresh cheetah poo, to be unpleasantly tolerable. Whippets, on the other paw, have extremely sensitive smell receptors and respond to the pungency of durian with a quick and astonishingly carrot–corn containing vomit.

That year, after the ceremonial throwing of the durian, as the whippets galloped around the track for the race's obligatory twelve and three-quarter laps, they vomited each time they passed the starting post where the durian had been thrown.

By lap six, rain had affected the track, turning it into a gluggy quagmire of mud, whippet vomit, and mashed durian. And as the dogs galloped through the muck at each turn, the muddy concoction was flung into the stands and even onto the royal boxes near the track.

Soon, the punters started to retch from the fragrant odour, the urge catching on in a contagious fashion.

By the time the whippets had run eleven and one-quarter laps, barely a metre of the track or stadium remained vomit-free.

The Mayor, who was traditionally honoured with a trackside seat, had been unfortunate enough to receive a great splattering of durian-whippet-vomit mud right in his cheering mouth, which made him immediately vomit onto the Royal Prince and Princess of the Lower Colon Counties, who were the guests of honour seated beside him.

That evening, he declared that exotic fruits would never again be permitted at the Winklebutty Cup, and the gherkin was immediately made the official, eternal and only vegetable suitable for jerking or tossing.

Meanwhile, Prince Cornbunkle of the Lower Colon Counties outlawed the harvesting of durian fruit, a decision that would later lead to an environmental catastrophe that pushed the lemmings and beavers of the region to the brink of extinction – a calamity the author in no way wishes to minimise despite it not being the main focus of this story.

This unfortunate incident would lead to the formation of a radical conservation movement called the Furious Durians, whose not-quite-rhyming and lopsided slogan was, 'Beavers, don't leave us! Beavers, don't leave us! Lemmings!'

CHAPTER 31
YEETING THE PICKLE

Phil Schiessenburger stood near-motionless on the starting dais. His right hand was clenched tight, and his left clutched a slightly larger than usual brown gherkin. He raised his hand halfway into the air, and the crowd fell silent with anticipation.

The tension was palpable, the air so thick you could cut it with a butter knife, assuming you had one in your possession and cutting thin (or thick) air was the sort of thing you tended to do. There seems no practical reason to attempt to slice air with any piece of cutlery, despite it being scientifically possible and only indirectly relevant to our story.

On the starting line, twenty-seven of the world's fastest-ever racing whippets quivered in a row. Well, maybe it was closer to twenty, given that not all the whippets were that fast.

Tradition required each borough to present their three speediest dogs. As there were nine boroughs ... well, you do the math(s) – or ask Rex or Destiny to do it for you.

Despite the thriving racing industry of the Lower Colon Colonies, not all boroughs had quick whippets. The borough of Little Tinkle was primarily inhabited by porcupines and weasels, so any whippets there were too busy trying to avoid porcupine practical jokes or unsolicited games of Whippet Pincushion to focus on racing.

Tradition, however, demanded that each borough provide its 'three finest' – a decree also inscribed on the mountain-goat-colon parchment.

If a borough had no decent dogs, it would invite retired whippets to race. They were not expected to win, or even to finish. As long as they lined up and completed one lap without passing out or vomiting, the borough's honour was maintained.

Completing a lap was important because the whippets and jockeys received payment for the race only if they finished at least one circuit. As soon as the race began, they would pull a muscle or break a leg, all stoically pushing through the pain to finish the first lap before collapsing on the racetrack.

The crowd would cheer, the borough's honour was maintained, and the fastest or most hepped-up whippet would win.

It was clearly a terrible year for 'honour', with many boroughs struggling to fill their three places.

This year, Ethyl Winklepimple, even at 88 years of age, was not only the oldest whippet in the race, but – according to the Winklebutty Bigbooty Museum and Burlesque Cabaret Restaurant's *Big Book of Racing Records* – was also the oldest surviving whippet in the region. She was racing purely to make up the numbers, but also because she felt terrible about exposing The Last Lap's financial strain to the *Lumpy Bottom Examiner*, a transgression for which Angeli Cup was still ignoring her.

A particularly nasty water tobogganing accident had also befallen the whippet sporting fraternity, putting three of the favourites from the regions in hospital.

High Hopes for Easter and Calamity at the Rodeo both had to withdraw due to injuries, while Frangipanni's Fluff remains, at the time of writing, in an induced coma at the Stanky Toe

Hospital for Racing Injuries. These are, understandably, serious tragedies, and the author wishes these athletes a speedy recovery.

Fortunately for The Last Lap, however, the unforeseen events had greatly improved Destiny's chance of maintaining her winning race record.

Despite Fate's Fur Art remaining the firm favourite, Destiny's Poo and Late Afternoon Glory had firmed to equal second favourites.

CHAPTER 32

AND THEY'RE OFF AND RACING!

As the gherkin and the racing track met, so the whippets sprang into action. The gentle pitter-patter of twenty-seven whippets galloping around the track on four legs (well, all except Ethyl Winklepimple, who had lost one leg in a game of Whippet Pincushion gone wrong, which had ended her career many years ago, so ... you do the maths) sounded much like a pasta dish straining through a colander. To others, it sounded like two pillows colliding, which is odd, because colanders and pillows make very different sounds. No matter the sound, the scent of freshly tossed gherkin always plunged everyone into a frenzied state of racing excitement.

The announcer would, in keeping with time-honoured tradition, whisper the dog's names rapid-fire in a controlled, unemotional voice.

The race was always accompanied by a popular music group designed to keep the crowd entertained during the preliminary races. This year, the Whistling Nostril Accordion Ensemble, led by world-renowned musician Claus Clapper, was blaring out their unique style of Oompah music.

Meanwhile, out on the racetrack, Fate's Fur Art had started as you might expect – like a rocket.

Destiny and Rex could do nothing about that. Cheetahs are sprinters that are naturally faster than whippets, a lot faster. Destiny knew her role was to not fall too far behind. As the race progressed, she could use her endurance and technique to overtake him.

Rex was an intuitive jockey. He never spoke or raised his hand. Although Rex was inexperienced, he and Destiny moved together as one, and he was lighter than Sally-Dee was for Destiny's older frame, which made a huge difference. Most of all, Rex was streamlined and aerodynamic. His shiny quills, when gelled back, had low drag while still creating enough downforce to improve his cornering. He didn't even use a whip. He did not need one. If he wanted Destiny to go faster, he would simply invert one of his lower spikes and jab her right in the small part of her butt that wasn't impervious to his spines – an encouragement more subtle and elegant than a whip, but twice as effective.

Even though Destiny could not smell a thing, with Rex riding her, it did not matter.

Somehow, she had reclaimed her passion.

Her paws moved with perfect precision, her timing in perfect synchronicity with Rex's movements. She picked up speed. She had all the motivation she needed to save The Last Lap, a far stronger incentive than all the stinky cheese in the counties.

After falling behind in the first five laps, Destiny and Rex were starting to close the distance. Fate's Fur Art's initial speed slowed, as he had to deal with Chad on his back. Fate's Fur Art found Chad to be lazier and stupider than an Indian Cheetah, so he ignored his jockey and whatever was going on around him and focused on the track.

To be fair, Chad was the only reason Melville hadn't won more races, which might have alerted authorities to his ruse. The pack of whippets hurtled past Fungus Foot Bend, entering the penultimate lap.

Destiny's Poo and Rex had caught up to Fate's Fur Art, who was now struggling with the excessive weight and unreliable balance of Chad's bloated rump.

Standard whippet races are usually only eleven and one-quarter laps, but for the spectacle of the Winklebutty Cup, a further and one and a half laps were added to squeeze in as many sponsorship and television advertisements as possible. This additional length would result in a small but important advantage for Destiny.

She edged ahead by a nose.

Then by an ear.

And then by two noses, and finally by a tail.

The crowd screamed and waved their hands as the excitement built.

Fate was spent. Cheetahs are not pack animals. They are ill-designed for hauling jockeys around a track, especially plump, uncoordinated ones. Destiny and Rex had worn Fate's Fur Art down and outrun him. They had ridden a better race; they deserved the win. But Chad was not done – no, not just yet.

Chattanooga Chad hadn't become the second five-time-winning whippet jockey of the Winklebutty Cup without having devious tricks up his sleeve.

Grabbing Fate's Fur Art's collar, he whispered, "Get ready to attack, you lazy, dumb cat." His instructions appeared to almost rhyme, as Chad was too lazy to make them actually rhyme, and as the rhyme would not, under most circumstances, influence the outcome of the race in any way. Rhyming, however poorly, was, after all, not illegal in whippet racing, although it was generally frowned upon almost everywhere else.

Cheetahs, it should also be noted, are aggressive, angry animals. Fate's Fur Art had been trained to attack rivals on command. He was clever enough to always do it on the last turn of the race, out of view of the crowd.

"Bite her, NOW!" yelled Chad, or that was what he had intended to yell. If he had, Fate's Fur Art would have bitten Destiny on the thigh, all but guaranteeing the cheetah's victory. Unfortunately, Chad had a tendency to mumble, so what he yelled and what Fate's Fur Art heard were two very different things.

Fate's Fur Art heard something closer to, "Bite 'em, NOW!" which to a Cheetah sounded much like, "Bite him, NOW!" or "Bite them, NOW!" Either instruction seemed plausible, as Chad had overemphasised the necessity to bite urgently while failing to pay due care and attention to the precise use of gender pronouns.

He had taken it for granted that Fate's Fur Art would bite Destiny, since biting Rex would be an obviously daft thing to do.

At this stage, it should be noted that cheetahs, while vicious and stupid, are sticklers for semantics. They will follow orders to the letter or not at all. Fate's Fur Art had never met Rex or Destiny, so he had no real way to assess their gender identities or their preferred use of pronouns. He was aware that Destiny was a biological female and Rex a biological male, but he did not feel it was his role to speculate on their pronouns at a time when all his mental energy should be focused on running and simultaneously biting ... *someone*.

Traditionally, depending on how the race was going, Chad instructed him to "Bite the whippet!" or "Bite the jockey!" both of which seemed much clearer, more precise commands.

Fate's Fur Art found himself trapped in a rare moment of indecision. The instruction to, "Bite 'em, NOW!" seemed more nuanced the more he thought about it.

Taken literally, the instruction suggested Chad wanted him to bite Rex, rather than Destiny, or maybe bite both Rex and Destiny.

The cheetah noted that Rex was, in fact, a porcupine, so biting him seemed unlikely to induce a positive result. To Fate's tiny cheetah brain, biting Destiny right in the rump seemed a wiser approach. Having bitten other whippets in the thigh, he had learnt to expect them to tumble over, allowing him to easily win.

Nonetheless, it was not a mount's role to question its rider. If Chattanooga Chad wanted him to bite a small, very prickly, and not at all tasty porcupine, that was what Fate's Fur Art would do. Heck, maybe Rex wasn't even a porcupine but a harmless small brown pillow, or a chicken drumstick dressed as a porcupine.

Surely, Fate's Fur Art thought, *my jockey has taken these facts into consideration when instructing me to bite the porcupine rather than the whippet.*

The very moment Fate's Fur Art bit into Rex, he heard, "Noooooo, you nincompoop! The whippet, not the porcupine!"

Realising his error, Chad had yelled to provide clarity on his previously imprecise instruction.

Fate's Fur Art, meanwhile, was surprised to find that Rex didn't taste at all like chicken. He tasked like a porcupine with lots of sharp, spiky spines and cheetah blood for seasoning.

As Rex's quills pierced through the cheetah's tongue and cheeks, Fate's Fur Art gave an ear-splitting shriek. He and Chad tumbled through the last corner, striking Phil Schiessenburger, who was waving the chequered flag.

Destiny and Rex cruised over the finish line a length ahead of a tumbling Chad on Fate's Fur Art, followed by Foot Fungus Fromage limping home in third position.

CHAPTER 33
PERFORMANCE ENHANCING MUSHROOMS

Angeli and Sally-Dee rushed onto the track to hug Destiny and high-five Rex. They were already being surrounded by members of the press, keen for a scoop.

"You did it. You really did it! I can't believe it." Angeli couldn't contain her emotions.

Destiny was overcome with joy, but she was too tired to even speak. Her tail was almost wagging – a not-too-subtle expression of whippet pride and excitement.

"Now, don't overdo it," Angeli Cup scolded. "Be a good winner."

"First ever porcupine jockey to win. How do you feel?" a reporter yelled at Destiny and Rex.

Rex wiggled two of his side spines, demonstrating the porcupine equivalent of false modesty.

"Oh, Rex didn't really do anything. Destiny was the real hero," interrupted Angeli.

The journalist, unfortunately, failed to notice Rex's two side spines and quoted Angeli literally.

"WHIPPET EARNS VICTORY WHILE PORCUPINE SHAMEFULLY ADMITS TO DOING NOTHING," the headline of the *Potters Crumpy Porcupine Weekly* announced online immediately after the race, before the rag apologised and retracted the story a short time later.

At that stage, Rex was not yet aware how the rest of the week would turn out; had he been, he would most certainly not have been anywhere near as excited as he appeared to be at that moment. He had not the slightest inkling that in twenty-four hours he would find himself in a police cell charged with attempted murder – and that wasn't even the really bad bit!

"Congratulations," Phil Schiessenburger beamed, revealing his ultra-white teeth. He had somehow managed to weave between the reporters to give Angeli a hug. He did not give Rex a hug. "You did it! Come with me up to the podium."

He approached the microphone. "Ladies, gentlemen, and various mammals and marsupials."

The crowd roared. Phil moved his hands in a downwards motion, his palms facing down. The crowd became quiet.

"It is my privilege to announce the winner of the 113th Winklebutty Cup, after a brief word from our chief sponsor, Fungaway. It is the only cream I trust to soothe my creamy parts." He leaned towards Destiny, holding his hand over his mouth. "Enjoy the victory, you earnt it."

"And now I will announce our winner, right after the compulsory drug test. As long as Destiny has not taken any PEMs, she will be awarded the victory." Phil placed his right arm in his trouser pocket and pulled out a large white lollipop-looking thing.

The crowd made a sort of whispering, murmuring sound that sounded like a group of bees talking to a slightly smaller group of growling chickens.

"What's this?" Angeli Cup ran up and placed herself between Phil and Destiny.

"I'm sorry, but the Board has decided to drug test the winner. Have to make sure there's no cheating, you know. Cup rules." Phil looked at Angeli. "I'm sorry, new rules. I didn't want to, but the Board insisted. You know how insistent they can be."

"But you are the head of the Board."

"Angeli, don't make this hard." Phil shrugged his shoulders and smiled. "Rules are rules."

He was correct, of course. Rule 18.1 stated that no rider or whippet could race under the influence of any performance enhancing mushrooms. The rule also stated that no jockey should wear crimson underwear. Never in the history of the Cup had these rules ever been enforced, however. Indeed, it was well known that most of the whippets were taking some form of performance enhancers, ranging from dogtosterone mushrooms to amphetacheese.

And as for underwear, it was unclear why Lord Winklebutty had written this particular rule on the goat-colon parchment. It was thought to relate to an unsuccessful romantic affair he had embarked upon with a pirate, although that was mostly speculation.

Phil handed the whippet the drug-testing paddle-pop stick, which Destiny licked three times.

"Now, if you have taken any performance enhancer, the stick will turn blue and you will be disqualified. If you are clean, it will turn red. If you are pregnant, it will turn green. I don't think that will get you disqualified, but I imagine you will get a stern talking to from your mum." Phil chuckled. The crowd didn't. Accidental pregnancy is no laughing matter.

Members of the organisation CAFEO (Cats and Felines Easily Offended), would go on to make complaints on social media about Phil's hurtful, insensitive joke about unborn but very real animals (UBVRAs) – the new term for what had previously been known as a foetus.

CAFEO members had been actively protesting the use of offensive words. Last year, they were able to ban the use of the words 'catnip', 'catawampus', 'caterpillar' and 'pussy willow' in all primary schools across the Middle Colon Counties.

This year, the coveted prized for Offensive Word of the Year went to the word 'catastrophe', which was clearly offensive to felines as it implied they were responsible for disasters. Having worked hard to dispel myths about black cats being bad luck, this word was seen as oppressive and insensitive.

CAFEO was also actively involved in dispelling misinformation about cats, such as that they always land on their feet and that they have nine lives. The myths were 'baseless claims' and 'conspiracy theories' that had been proved completely incorrect, lacking any foundation, and mostly false by cat-checkers at CAFEO.

Research by scientists from the Winklebutty Health Organisation, who had published their findings in an award-winning expose on cat agility in the prestigious *Winklebutty Science Monthly*, demonstrated that cats do not always land on their feet when falling.

Six months earlier, eight-year-old primary school student Maggie McTubbin had already established that the first myth was untrue, using only a third-story window and her pussy cat, Muffin. As for the myth about cats having nine lives, well the jury is still out at the time of writing, although most legal experts expect a guilty verdict. The experiment still haunts Miss McTubbin to this day.

Meanwhile, back at the racetrack, Rex looked nervous. If it was at all possible for a porcupine to look nervous, this would have been a fair assessment of his emotional state, which was very anxious indeed.

Phil looked at Angeli Cup. Half of his face smiled a half

smile and the other a half grimace, as if his face was undecided as to what it was meant to do.

Destiny's tail wagged in a fast, clockwise motion. Such a motion meant fear, and everyone knew it. The crowd let out a slight 'awwwww' type sound.

Phil's face made up its mind and decided to smile. He approached the microphone and addressed the crowd. "I'm afraid to announce the drug test is ..." He stared down at the testing stick. His face replaced its smile with a slight frown. "Well, it's, err. It's ... it's green!"

An immediate roar sprang from the crowd. Angeli Cup ran to Destiny and hugged her tightly. "For a moment, I thought you might have taken the dogtosterone," she murmured.

Destiny smiled and wagged her tail to the left.

Angeli Cup chuckled. "Yes, yes, you are the GOAT of whippet racing, after all."

Phil ambled over to Destiny. "Congratulations, Destiny. I never had a doubt." He looked at Angeli and smiled. "You really should have more faith in her." Then he turned back to the crowd. "Ladies and gentlemen, this year's winner of the 113th Winklebutty Cup is Destiny's Poo, ridden by Rex."

CHAPTER 34

TO THE WINNERS GO THE SPOILS

"So, The Last Lap is safe now. We can come over and pay the m-mortgage after the ceremony," Angie stammered as the crowd roared out its applause.

Phil smiled. "Don't worry about that. I'll sort it out later." He turned towards Destiny and Rex. In his right hand, he held an original Winklebutty Cup replica. "To the winners go the spoils..." Turning, he gave Angeli a firm hug. "Now, cousin. Come get your cheese."

Phil strode up to the stairs to the ceremonial podium, towing Angeli Cup behind him along with Rex and Destiny.

"Since when do trainers get to eat the cheese, too?" Angeli raised her eyebrows.

"Since now. New rules. The winning trainer gets to eat the cheese in equal amounts, especially if the jockey is a porcupine." He smiled at Angeli and winked as he ushered her up to the podium, too. "And remember, rules are rules."

Angeli blushed. "Thanks, Phil. I could not have done it without you."

"Hey, that's what family is for. Enjoy your victory. I'll go straight to the bank afterwards and prepare the paperwork."

Rex and Destiny proudly trod the purple carpet towards the

ceremonial plate. Phil placed the cheese platter on the ceremonial plinth while the Mayor of Winklebutty approached the lectern.

"I am pleased to announce that the winner of the 113th Winklebutty Cup is Dest—"

"STOP! I OBJECT!" Chad Cheerio marched to the podium. In his right hand, he clutched a weighty leather-bound book. Next to him, wearing a grey tweed suit, stood a medium-sized person whose identity would become obvious in a few seconds.

The crowd murmured and muttered to themselves momentarily before they were interrupted.

"I'm Mr David Dill, no relationship to any pickles or gherkins," the interjector said, approaching the Mayor. "This person has cheated." He waved his arms across his chest three times before pointing his index finger at Destiny and possibly at Rex. It was difficult to work out who he was pointing at, which depended on the direction from which you viewed the scene. To me, it looked like he was pointing at Destiny, but I can see how someone might see it differently if they were watching the scene from the very cheap and often muddy seats in the front rows, still referred to as 'Durian Drag'.

"The rules are clear," the man insisted. "No sharp spikes or poking instruments are allowed to be used by the jockey – Rule 117c." He raised the leather-bound book and pointed to one of the pages. It was hard to tell exactly which paragraph he was pointing at, but let's assume it was to rule 117c.

The Mayor took the book and mumbled to himself for a few minutes. Turning to another officious-looking official, he mumbled to him. After a few minutes of muttering, he strode towards a microphone near the lectern. "Ahem ... according to rule 117c, I announce that Destiny's Poo and Rex the porcupine are disqualified."

The crowd gave a loud 'oooohh' sound. Rex gave a near imperceptible fart sound. And Destiny gave a small but extremely exasperated sigh, because – as an astute reader will remember – her butt was *almost* entirely impervious to Rex's poking, so all the spiking in the world could not have affected her natural desire to race her best.

"I announce the winners of the 113th Winklebutty Cup to be Fate's Fur Art and Chad Cheerio."

The crowd made another 'oooohh' sound.

Chad and Fate's Fur Art darted onto the winner block. "Ha! Suck on this, Angeli 'Crappy Copper' Cup!" Chad grabbed the cheese from its plinth before Phil could even offer it to him and shoved all of it into his gob in a single swift motion. "Six times winner. Six times winner! Six ... times ..." he mumbled, cheesily.

"What have you done, you fool?" Phil muttered and shook his head as he scurried from the podium.

Sally-Dee and Angeli stood motionless and speechless. Turning, they stared at each other, mouths agape. There was nothing to say.

And then, with an ear-splitting bang, everything went dark.

CHAPTER 35
THE AFTERMATH

Destiny shock her head a few times and slowly rose to her feet. Sally-Dee and Angeli Cup did the same. Rex also climbed to his feet, although, to the untrained eye, it wouldn't have been evident he had ever fallen off his feet in the first place.

Around them, a thick, smoky fog was lifting, making the scene of devastation before them more evident. The podium was shattered, and punters everywhere were crawling back to a vertical position. It was clear there had been an explosion of some sort.

Fate's Fur Art stumbled to his paws, mostly unharmed.

"What the blazes! What sort of whippet is this?" The Mayor looked shocked.

The explosion had blown off much of the winner's paint and make-up, revealing the unmistakeable black spots and yellow markings usually associated with ... cheetahs.

"This is clearly a cheetah, which is clearly also against the rules. Chad and Fate's Fur Art, you are also disqualified. Er, I guess that makes the winner Foot Fungus Fromage. And you, Fate's Fur Art – if that is your real name – should be ashamed of yourself. You are not a whippet!"

Melville, which was Fate's Fur Art's real name, hung his head low and crawled away in shame. He was sad – very sad. It wasn't losing the Cup that mattered to him. He'd never actually cared about winning. Nor was it that he'd been caught cheating, since there is no shame in being caught doing what you are designed to do. But to be told that he was not a whippet hurt. Maybe Melville was not born a whippet, but in his heart, more than anything, a racing whippet was all he wanted to be.

Sirens sounded as the Winklebutty First Response Services poured into the racing ground. Ambulance workers rushed to tend to the injured. Thankfully, aside from a few sprained ankles and bruised hips, there were no other serious injuries and, fortunately, no fatalities. Eventually, Chad Cheerio was located and was immediately rushed to the emergency department of the Stanky Toe Hospital for Racing Injuries.

CHAPTER 36

INDESCRIBABLE AGONY

At the other end of a large white hospital bed was a young man with what appeared to be a red pumpkin stuck on his head. I say *appeared*, because it was, of course, not a pumpkin. The man was a patient at Stanky Toe Hospital for Racing Injuries, and it was against the Hypocritical Oath for doctors to stick red pumpkins on the heads of their patients. As a general principal, this rule was adhered to most of the time, but there are always exceptions to any rule. In this situation, the exception was the very swollen, but still unmistakable face of Chad Cheerio.

Sally-Dee stood on one side of the bed, beside the intensive care specialist, Dr Putz, with Destiny on the other side, already looking somewhat bored.

"Is he alive?" Sally asked, staring despite herself.

"Well, yes. He'd be downstairs in the morgue on G floor if he were dead." Dr Putz chuckled. "It's bad for morale to leave dead people in the ward." The doctor's voice dropped to a whisper. "Tends to scare the punters and cause a penetrating smell that is surprisingly hard to shift."

An awkward silence followed.

"Will he pull through, Dr Putz?"

"No idea! But if he doesn't, you can guarantee we'll get him down to G floor in a jiffy. Our wardsman is very efficient. Only last week, we had a punter who died from a toe fungus infection. Our wardsman got him to G floor in two minutes and seventeen seconds. That's a district record, you know."

Another silence.

"He's very lucky to be alive," Dr Putz continued, pulling Chad's chart off the end of the bed and flipping through the pages distractedly. "You see, the Lumpy Bottom lava pepper is a very potent chilli. Of course, dogs have cast-iron stomachs. If a whippet eats a lava pepper, well, all that happens is that they lose their sense of smell."

"It damages their nose?" Sally-Dee queried, wrinkling hers. "Like it did Destiny's?"

"Yep! That's where the burn exits in dogs. Not too much damage that way, although most dogs will never smell again. In humans, however, the Lumpy Bottom lava pepper does most of its damage when it comes out. It's so hot it will ignite any methane in your bowel. The pressure builds and builds, and then, when it can't escape, well ... you know ..." The doctor's eyebrows waggled.

"Well, what?"

"Kaboom!" Dr Putz suddenly jumped up and down, making mad circling hand motions. "The only way to save them is to let the gas out early, before they pop."

"And how do you let it out?"

"Passing wind, of course. It's the only way to survive Lumpy Bottom lava pepper ingestion."

"Passing wind." Sally considered it for a second. "Doesn't sound too hard."

"Not hard, but it does make a mess. Luckily, Chad was able to pass wind just before his intestines reached terminal pressure. It saved his life, but it sure made a fiery mess."

"A hot mess?"

"Yes, think of it this way. Passing wind from a Lumpy Bottom lava pepper is like pooping lava. Your butt gets burnt from the inside. It's like having a pizza oven in your rectum and setting it to 2 billion degrees, and then letting three large tubs of cheese ignite in it—"

"Oh, I think I get the picture," Sally-Dee interrupted.

Dr Putz pulled out the chart and flicked through the notes. "Nasty. Looks like he lost all of his right butt cheek – blown clean off. Bits of it landed in Potters Crumpy. Struck an elderly woman on the head. Knocked her out."

"Ouch." Sally cringed. "Painful!"

"Not at all. She didn't know what hit her. She was playing outdoor bowls at the time," Dr Putz explained. "She woke up in hospital and didn't remember a thing. She's made a full recovery. It took a little while to get all the pieces of butt cheek out of her hair, though. Last I heard, she was back bowling."

"How about Chad?"

"Mr Cheerio? Not so lucky. He has fifth-degree burns to what's left of his other butt cheek."

"Fifth-degree burns? I thought third-degree were the worst burns you could get?"

"Ha, ha, ha," Putz chortled. "For ordinary fire burns, yes. But lava pepper burns have two extra degrees of burn."

"So, even more painful?"

Ha, ha, ha," Putz laughed again. "Not just painful. It's indescribable agony. Imagine your friend Rex, here ..." Dr Putz pointed at the porcupine, who looked none too happy about where this was heading. "Imagine covering him with hydrochloric acid, extra hot Tabasco sauce, petrol, and a topping of lava, and then showing him—"

"I thought you said the pain was indescribable. That seems a pretty good description."

Rex disagreed. He thought it was a totally stupid description.

Beep, Beep, Beep... An alarm sounded, interrupting Dr Putz as the door opened and a hefty male nurse strolled in.

"Will Chad ever ride again?" Sally-Dee queried.

"Ha, ha, ha. You make me laugh." Dr Putz grinned. "Ride? Not a chance. He'll be lucky if he can ever sit again. And even if he can, he will always sit crooked. I mean, he could get a cheek implant, but I really don't recommend that. Implants are quite temperamental and have a tendency to explode, too. No, his riding days are well behind him – much like his right butt cheek down in lower Potter's Crumpy."

The male nurse rolled a stainless-steel trolly close to Chad's bed. On it was a large jar of green and brown sludge. Next to that was a long glass syringe the size of a small oxygen tank, and next to that was a needle the size of a small baseball bat.

"Would you give us some privacy, please." The nurse turned to Sally and Dr Putz. "He needs his R and R now." He drew the curtains.

Dr Putz strode to the other end of the room, motioning for Sally to follow. Unusual squelching sounds came from behind the curtain, followed by faint screaming.

What's R and R?" Sally asked. "Rest and recuperation?"

"Oh no. Rectal rehabilitation."

Sally shuddered. "What does *that* involve?"

"You don't want to know!"

A crooked smile formed on Sally-Dee's face as she walked towards the door. When she reached it, she turned around. "Dr Putz, what time do you finish?"

"Err, in about an hour, I hope."

Would you like to grab a pizza and soda at The Fox and Whippet once you're done? It's two for the price of one tonight."

"I would." Dr Putz smiled, and even blushed a little. "But I'm not allowed to fraternise with patients, their relatives, or their friends."

"Well, I'm none of those things."

"I thought you were Chad's girlfriend."

"God no! I'd sooner eat porcupine vomit."

Rex growled in disapproval. He wiggled three of his lower spines, making it abundantly clear that he did not at all appreciate Sally-Dee using cheap porcupine metaphors when trying to flirt with doctors. Sally-Dee was too busy flirting with Dr Putz to notice.

"Oh no, Dr Putz, I'm his sporting rival," Sally confessed. I just wanted to check on him. Sporting etiquette, you know."

"Well, in that case, I'd love to have dinner with you, Sally."

"Great! I'll book a table, Dr Putz."

"Oh Sally, don't be so formal. Call me Penelope."

CHAPTER 37
ARREST THE PORCUPINE

Penelope Putz mumbled to herself as she wrote in her medical file. She put the folder back on the end of the bed, where Chad Cheerio was lying unconscious.

"All done! Let's get that drink." She smiled at Sally-Dee, who smiled back.

Rex did not smile; instead, he placed his right front paw down his throat, pretending to make himself throw up.

"Don't be so jealous" Sally chided him.

"Well, well, well, what have we here?" came a familiar voice. "Constable Olivia Oregano and Officer Paul Pavlova first at the scene it appears. Not trying to run from the law, I hope, Mr Spikington," Constable Oregano said in a voice that was firm like gravel. She stared down at Rex and grimaced. Presumably, her voice did the same.

"What seems to be the problem, Officer?" Sally-Dee asked.

"No problem. No problem at all. Just doing police work – good police work," Constable Oregano added menacingly, raising her eyebrows. "I smell something very fishy going on here."

"Well, that could be the bouillabaisse from last night," Dr Putz interrupted.

Constable Oregano gestured to Sally-Dee. "I might just ask Chad's *sporting rival* here a few questions. Seems to me you disliked Chattanooga Chad, didn't you, Ms Pickles? Is that why you had the porcupine *murder* him?"

Officer Pavlova tapped his partner on the shoulder, pointed toward the curtain surrounding Chad Cheerio's bed. He whispered in her ear.

"Well, that's very bad news," Constable Oregano replied. She walked over to the hospital bed and prodded Chad with her police truncheon. "He looks pretty dead to me. Are you sure he's alive?" She turned her attention back to Sally-Dee and Rex. "So, did you think Mr Cheerio messed with your saddle? Is that why you had this porcupine very seriously almost kill him by stabbing?"

Officer Pavlova whispered in her ear again.

"Oh, really?" Constable Oregano replied. "Well, in that case, is that why you had this porcupine sabotage the victory cheese to try to kill him?"

Sally-Dee looked between the doctor and the police officers incredulously. "Don't be ridiculous! It was Rocco Parmigiana who poisoned him! He made the cheese, not Rex. And he's been trying to get his hands on The Last Lap for years."

Constable Olivia Oregano tapped the side of her nose. "Hearsay I would say." She walked back over to Rex and pointed at him "So, why would the most successful business owner Lumpy Bottom has ever known destroy his own name and poison his own nephew? His very famous jockey nephew, on whom he had bet heavily to win. Seems he lost a small fortune from the exploding cheese debacle.

"He wasn't trying to kill Chad. He was trying to kill us!" Sally-Dee pointed to herself and Rex.

"How about we let a judge decide," Olivia declared. "Book 'em," she instructed Sergeant Pavlova, who looked between Sally-Dee and Rex in a confused manner.

He cleared his throat. "Ah, 'em?"

"Book 'em. Book *him*! The porcupine! And her, the jockey!" Constable Oregano declared. "Rex Spikington, you're under arrest for the injuring of one Chad Cheerio. Ms Sally-Dee Pickles, you're also under arrest for helping the porcupine injure the same Chad Cheerio. You are an accessory to the crime. Or it could be accessary, I always get those two mixed up".

"Does it really make a difference?" Dr Putz snapped.

"Well," Constable Oregano continued. "One is a legal term for a person who assisted with a crime, which Sally most definitely did. The other refers to an item that can be added to another thing to make it more useful. It is fair to say that does not accurately describe Sally at all. So, yes, I want to be precise with my words."

Penelope stepped forward. "That is mean and unnecessary. Besides, Sally was with me the whole time. She could not possibly have been involved. I can vouch for Ms Pickles. Look at the state of her." Dr Putz motioned to Sally-Dee's cast. "She was with me at the hospital the entire time. Medical emergency. It's a watertight alibi."

"With you? Here at the hospital?" Officer Oregano narrowed her eyes.

"Yes, she contracted a very bad case of ... ah ... cheesy foot fungus."

Both police officers took a step back and wrinkled their noses.

"Yes! Seriously septic stanky toe. Worse case I've ever seen. Or rather stanky leg, even. Not even Fungaway helped. It got into her cast, and it spread all the way up to her crutches. Most rancid pus I have ever seen. Funny thing is when infected pus mixes with a cheese fungus infection it creates a smell so disgusting that even—"

Sergeant Pavlova put a hand over his mouth. "Thanks, but that's quite enough detail, Doctor."

Constable Oregano looked at Pavlova and shook her head. "Well, I don't care about the girl. She annoys me, but I'm arresting the porcupine." She pulled a pair of small, shiny handcuffs off her police belt and snapped them around Rex's tiny paws. "Nathaniel John Spikington Junior, you are under arrest, and you are stupid and annoying."

Sergeant Pavlova tapped her on the shoulder again and whispered loudly, "That's not what we say here."

"Fine," she spat. "You are just under arrest. About the 'being stupid' thing, well just read between the lines. I'm not saying you *are* stupid, but I can't prove you're not. You are definitely annoying, though." She turned her head toward Pavlova and turned the palms of her hands upwards."

Sergeant Pavlova shook his head again and shrugged.

"In any case, you're coming with us. You can come quietly, or you can come screaming due to me smacking you with my truncheon," snarled Officer Oregano. Sergeant Pavlova sighed and again shook his head.

Sally-Dee got up to hobble after them, but Officer Oregano stopped her at the door. "Not you, Pickles." She waved a black truncheon at Sally's cast. "You stay here and clear up that little ... stanky leg issue." She turned to Dr Putz. "Doctor, thank you for your time. We will be in touch if we require a written statement."

"Of course. I'm a doctor. I am renowned for my penmanship."

Officer Oregano cleared her throat and made a hmmpfff sound as she dragged a solemn-looking Rex towards the door.

"Or penwomanship," Sally-Dee added. She looked at Rex. "And maybe penporcupineship or penwippetship, or—"

"—shut up!" Oregano interrupted.

Dr Putz shrugged as the two police officers exited with Rex through the sliding glass doors.

“Don’t worry, Rex. We’ll get to the bottom of this!” Sally-Dee yelled after him.

“Ouch!” grimaced Penelope as they faded from sight. “That was nasty.”

Sally-Dee collapsed into a chair and clutched her head. “Poor, Rex. This is all my fault. If only I hadn’t broken my leg. I’m a terrible whippet jockey, and an even worse friend.”

“Now, now,” Penelope patted her shoulder. “At least you don’t actually have stanky leg. It’s extremely contagious and very hard to cure.”

“Thank you for sticking up for me,” Sally mumbled. “We have to find a way to get Rex out. What should we do?”

“Well, let’s start with a pizza. That never hurts.”

CHAPTER 38

ANYTHING YOU SAY IS STUPID AND POINTLESS

Rex sat silently on a wooden bench at the East Potters Crumpy Police Station, his front paws restrained in steel handcuffs.

"You have the right to remain silent," Olivia Oregano said without blinking. She appeared to be smiling, but it was hard to be certain. "Anything you say is stupid and pointless, so do not bother. I've already decided you're guilty, so shut up."

Officer Pavlova tapped her on the shoulder and whispered to her once more.

"Are you sure?" Constable Oregano looked slightly puzzled.

She shrugged her shoulders and turned back to Rex. "Well, apparently, a jury gets to decide that you're guilty, not me." She crossed her arms over her chest.

Officer Pavlova tapped her again.

"Okay, okay! *If* you are guilty." She lowered her voice a little. "But we all know you done it."

Pavlova whispered again.

"We all know you *did* it." She looked at Pavlova and nodded. "Now, where was I? Oh, that's right – you have the right to shut your little mouth. Any sarcastic remarks from your spiky spines will be noted and used against you. You have the right to an attorney, but you can't afford one, you little weasel ..."

"Not so fast, Olivia!" A tallish man in a blue-striped suit glided across the vinyl floor of the police station towards her.

Olivia's almost-smile turned into a not-at-all-almost frown. Her mouth made the shape a mouth might make if it had just accidentally bitten into a lemon covered in hot English mustard.

"I'll be representing the ... weasel." The man pointed to Rex, who appeared even less happy than he had when he'd first arrived at the police station.

"Hold your horses, young man. I'm Officer Pavlova, and you can't just waltz into my police station without permission. Now, who exactly would you be? And what is your business here?" Officer Pavlova inquired.

"Ah, so, you must be the famed Constable Pavlova, the most decorated police officer in the Lower Colon Counties. Three times winner of Police Officer of the Year, and, if I'm not mistaken – which I never am – twice winner of the Loaded Durian Trophy for best undercover police work." The man held out his hand and moved towards Pavlova.

An awkward silence followed.

Pavlova glanced at Olivia, who glanced back.

"No, that's my brother. I'm Paul Pavlova."

"Oops, my bad! You must be proud of your brother –

smashing police officer! The 'Cheese Detective.' Gosh, the way he solved the Potters Crumpy Seafood Olympics affair was masterful. A true inspiration. I love his books. I've read every one of them. Do you think you could get me an autograph?"

Pavlova stared at the man unemotionally. He seemed to be copying Olivia's almost-smile. "No."

"Ah, fair enough. Must be hard to live in his shadow. Especially when he's so great, and you are so ... well ... *you* ..."

"So *what*?" Olivia interrupted. "Exactly *what* are you suggesting he is?"

"Well, it's just that he's no Officer Pavlova, is he? I mean, strictly speaking, he *is* Officer Pavlova. But he is not *the* Officer Pavlova, if you know what I mean."

"No! I don't know what you mean," Officer Pavlova stated abruptly, knowing exactly what the man meant.

Rex also knew what he meant, but he did not especially care. The handcuffs were digging into his tiny paws, which were already sore from the race. He was about to interject when he decided there was not much point. He didn't think any of them were interested in listening to him.

"Who are you?"

"Great question, Constable Oregano." The newcomer pointed at her. "Sharp as a tack, as always. That, I guess, is why you were voted Friendliest Police Officer three years running."

"That is my sister Ophelia."

"Ah, my bad. She's *very* friendly, your sister, *if you know what I mean*?" He winked at Olivia and scratched at his ear slightly. "Er, no, maybe you don't. Still, I guess the apple doesn't fall far from the tree, does it?"

"Who are you?"

"To the point – I like that in an officer. I'm Ace, Ace McBalls. I'm sure you've heard of me." The handsome interloper patted himself on his extremely well-muscled chest. "Author, self-help guru to the stars, and part-time defence attorney for the downtrodden and probably-not-guilty types. Please don't be intimidated by my fame. Deep down, I'm just an ordinary guy who happens to be exceedingly famous and outrageously talented and good-looking. My latest self-help book has just sold a tonne of copies. I mean a real truckload of books. It's titled—"

"Never meet your heroes," Angeli interrupted under her breath. "For someone so inspiring, you were lacklustre at the whippet racing hearings!"

"No need to thank me."

"I'm not. You were appalling. Really awful."

"Let's not dwell on the past, shall we? As I always say: Live the now, not the could-have-been. The important thing is that I'm a guru, and I'm *here*." Ace stalked over to Rex and patted him on the head a number of times. "So, what's the name of this spiky little weasel I'm defending?

CHAPTER 39
THE FOX AND WHIPPET

"You've hardly touched your pepperoni pizza." Penelope pointed to a healthy-looking, medium-sized pizza sitting right in front of Sally-Dee. In front of Penelope sat the much less healthy-looking remnant of what had, in its glory days, been a robust and well-baked cheese, tofu and leek pizza. Now, all that remained of it were two curved pieces of crust.

"I can't eat right now. Rex has been charged with sabotaging the cheese. He's in prison, and Angeli has been told he's been refused bail. Destiny has been disqualified from the race, and now the bank will repossess The Last Lap and Rocco Parmigiana will take it over." Sally-Dee was tapping her good foot as fast as it wanted to tap, which was fast for a human of her age but painfully slow to a racing whippet.

"Can I have it?"

"Have what? The Last Lap?"

"No. The pepperoni pizza."

"Have you listened to what I've said at all?"

"Sure. No point wasting pizza, though. That won't help the situation at all."

"Well, what would help the situation?"

"Why don't we pay Mr Parmigiana a little visit, see whether

he's willing to talk to us." Penelope smirked and punched her right fist into her left hand.

"I don't think he'll want to talk to us."

"Well, turns out I'm very persuasive." Penelope again punched her fist into her hand.

"How do you mean? Did you do debating or something?" Sally-Dee asked. Then she muttered under her breath, "I still don't think Rocco will talk to us."

Penelope rolled her eyes. "Read between the lines. I am *very* persuasive. Understand?"

"Not really."

Penelope dropped her voice an octave. "I'm going to punch him in the head until he talks," she said menacingly. "Is that clear enough for you?"

"Oh, I see. Not to be negative, but I don't think you can do that."

"Why? Because I'm a girl? You think I can't fight. Is that what you are saying? I'll have you know I'm a black belt in Kung Fu, *and* I'm the three-time Lower Colon Counties wrestling champion. I must say, I was not expecting that kind of bigotry from you, of all people." Penelope stood up and banged her fist on the table.

"Er, no ...! I just meant that I don't think it is *legal* to do that. It's probably against the law."

"Well, yes, fair enough." Penelope calmed down. "It probably isn't permitted, but neither is making up an alibi or poisoning the victory cheese. Anyway, what are our options? Are we just going to let Rocco get away with framing Rex for this, or are we prepared to fight, fight, fight?" She pumped her fist in the air three times.

Sally-Dee was momentarily distracted. On the other side of the bar, a large whippet had just slumped into a booth all by himself. On closer inspection, Sally-Dee realised it was Fate's Fur Art. Her eyes widened and a menacing look found its way onto her face. “What is he doing here?” she asked Penelope, jutting her chin in the cheetah’s direction.

“Only one way to find out.”

Before Sally-Dee could object, Penelope leapt out of her chair and marched to his table. “You’ve got a nerve, showing yourself here, you cheating cheetah cheater.” (At least that’s what I think she said, although she might have meant ‘cheating cheater cheetah’. I’m not sure it would make much difference.)

Penelope was expecting a fight, and she was ready for it. Sally-Dee was expecting a fight, too, and she was not ready for it at all.

Melville was expecting a drink. He just looked forlorn. He took a long swig of his cosmopolitan and sighed. And then, over the next hour, he told them everything.

CHAPTER 40
IS IT BECAUSE I'M A GIRL?

"Wow, that is a big sausage." Penelope sighed.

In front of them, not more than ten metres away, was the Lumpy Bottom Meat Emporium – the most secretive building in the Upper Boroughs and the third most secretive building in the entire district according to a recent survey conducted by the Potters Crumpy Secret Service, Security, and Seafood Safety Department.

Each year, the PC Quintuple S, as it was affectionately known, would review all the building of the districts and rate them according to their level of secrecy and security. It was considered a great honour to make the list, and an even greater honour to win.

An even greater honour than winning was to not make the list at all, because then your building was clearly so secretive and well-hidden that not even the PC Quintuple S knew it existed. This year, that honour went to the Potters Crumpy Local Government Complaints Department building.

The Meat Emporium was nowhere near as well hidden as the Complaints Department. The emporium had been built by Rocco Parmigiana at the beginning of his sausage boom and had been shrouded in secrecy, mystery and saucery ever since. (Well, not saucery, I made that up because it sort of, almost rhymed, and because meat does require a lot of sauces. To be honest, I'm not even totally certain 'saucery' is a real word, although 'sorcery' certainly is.)

The inner workings of the factory were known only to an inner sanctum of Rocco's closest, most trusted henchmen – and his mum. He had no friends, and he thought of his mum as one of the boys. Strictly speaking, the factory was therefore known only to his henchmen and henchwoman and possibly two henchporcupines. Attempts by animal rights groups to gain entry to the factory had all been foiled by protracted legal challenges.

From a short distance away, the building appeared completely featureless. Only from a closer distance could the letters of the LBME logo be seen, mostly because the black sausage on a black background covered in black sauce was impossible to see during sunny days or moonless nights. The moonlight on this particular evening, however, helped show the outline, which could be clearly deciphered – a salami sausage three metres wide and ten metres across, and then, over the sausage in small gothic letters, the company's motto: 'Some secrets are worth keeping.'

"How the heck do we get in?" Sally-Dee whispered.

Penelope raised her eyebrows. "Leave it to me. Unless you think I'm too weak to manage it because I'm a girl."

Sally-Dee did not respond.

Penelope opened a green hessian backpack and removed a long length of rope that ended in a large, sharp-looking metal hook. In a single fast motion, she hurled the hook, which flew almost elegantly to an open window about five metres above the ground. "I used to be a boy scout," she said. "I like to be prepared."

Sally-Dee looked at Rex, Rex stared at Melville, and Melville stared at Penelope and wagged his tail to the left.

"Something you want to say, Melville?" Penelope's face was stern.

Melville may only have been a small-brained cheetah, but he recognised that facial expression.

"Don't you think a girl can be a boy scout? Do you think I'm too weak or stupid because I'm a girl?" It was, of course, a rhetorical question – the type of question that can easily get you a punch in the mouth.

But Melville just shook his head vigorously. He hadn't been thinking that at all. He just thought it was odd that a doctor was carrying a grappling hook in her bag. He was also aware that Penelope had the same look in her eyes as the look of a South American rhinoceros just before it trampled an entire herd of smaller animals.

Melville tried to stay calm and nonchalantly raised his shoulder and left paw in a classic sign of, "Oh really? I hadn't even noticed you were a girl."

"What do you mean you didn't notice I was a girl?" Penelope screeched in her best impression of an exploding thing exploding.

Sally-Dee, meanwhile, had climbed the rope unnoticed and was already at the top of the window. "Oh, my goodness! Come up here, quick. You won't believe what's in here."

Penelope was distracted for a split second – just enough time for Melville to scamper up the rope to temporary safety. Penelope followed.

Farump... wallop ... crunch ... squelch – CLANK.

CLANK – CLUNK Farump ...wallop... crunch ... squelch. CLANK-CLANK-CLUNK.

The factory was illuminated by a dim red light, which made it hard to distinguish any other colours. The outline of the machines could be faintly seen, but it was impossible to judge depth or distance. The sound, however, was clearly coming from one direction.

"Let's go that way." Penelope pointed in a direction mostly unrelated to where the sound was coming from.

Melville, however, padded towards the sound.

"You know, Melville. In the red light, you really do look like a whippet."

Melville wagged his tail. He was flattered, but he was also too busy to respond. With every step, the squelching machine sounds intensified, until they reached a large, dark-green object.

It looks like a huge dog bowl, Sally-Dee thought. A large silver plunger was moving up and down in the bowl in close rhythm with the sound.

Melville rubbed the dirt and dust from a plaque on the side. 'Sausaginator Mark III' the plaque read.

"Sausaginator ... what the heck is that?" Penelope scoffed.

Seems self-explanatory, don't you think? Melville thought to himself, but he had the good judgment not to verbalise the thought.

"Sort of self-explanatory, don't you think?" Sally-Dee chortled, not having the judgment Melville had exercised.

"Yeah, I guess so." Penelope laughed.

Melville growled but again chose not to say what he was thinking.

Sally-Dee stood on her tiptoes and peered over the edge into the sausaginator. The silver plunger thingy was merrily squishing a brown gooey type of goo and some other chunky, unguessable object through a hole the size of a toilet bowl.

Sally-Dee reached into the bowl and scraped off some of the goo with two of her less popular fingers. "This must be the sausage stuffing," she announced.

Wow, I walk among the truly gifted, thought Melville, but once again, his small cheetah brain declined to say anything.

Sally-Dee sniffed her fingers and licked the goo, which made Melville gag involuntarily. He found her action truly gross, which, in truth, seems a bit judgemental from a species that considers rhino vomit a delicacy.

"It tastes like ... well ... I think it's *tofu*. Mushroom tofu, to be precise."

Sally-Dee looked at Penelope, who looked at Melville, who looked back at Sally-Dee and wondered what *tofu* was. He was hungry, so he was hoping Penelope might have some vomit in her hessian sack. She did not, but through an unusual twist of fate, that was about to change.

CHAPTER 41

A SHADOWY ENCOUNTER

Half an hour and a little bit earlier

Rocco Parmigiana had also been unaware that his fate was about to change. Typically, providence goes unnoticed by the average person, especially in Lumpy Bottom, until a string of coincidences makes them realise they've been seeing yellow cars their entire lives and only just now yelling "Spotto!" which must surely portend some deeper truth about the workings of the universe.

Rocco had been on the factory floor of the Meat Emporium, testing a new recipe for a batch of Premium Chihuahua Sausages when he had the unmistakable feeling that the hair was standing up on the back of his neck. Neck hair is generally not a pleasant thing, and neck-beards, particularly, are frowned upon almost universally – except for in Little Tinkle, where, when combined with a stylish cravat, they have become a popular symbol of gentrification. But at the Lumpy Bottom Meat Emporium, Rocco's hair was standing up in a way that suggested something very bad and very unexpected was about to happen.

The change in circumstances that had prompted Rocco's

neck hairs to start behaving autonomously was the introduction to his working space of a large, man-shaped shadow.

It is possible to argue that a man-shaped shadow might not be the scariest of shadows you could have the misfortune to cross paths with. But it is an argument that will not win you many friends.

The bears of the Potters Crumpy Pig and-Poke-a-Bear-Fair would argue that their shadows are, or should be, much scarier. Even the pigs might insist that pigs are far from harmless either and that the shadow of their Razorback ancestors should instil the kind of fingernail-biting terror that CGI 1980s-era horror movies do today. But in this case, the man-shaped shadow was a *very large* man-shaped shadow. And the shape of Rocco Parmigiana, as you will remember, was of a very small man.

Rocco shivered and then bravely spun to face his much-larger adversary. But there was no one there. Clearly, the shadow, and the very large man who had thrown it, had slunk back against the wall, possibly gearing up to throw another shadow. Shadow-throwing is not a common sport in the Lower Colon Countries or even in the Upper Boroughs, as it takes some knack to get it right.

A tremor of terror rattled through Rocco Parmigiana's short and rather brittle bones at the thought of another shadow encroaching.

As an astute reader, you might guess that, following the events of the 113th Winklebutty Cup, Rocco Parmigiana had been expecting a visit from the constabulary. In fact, given his unorthodox business practices, Rocco Parmigiana had been expecting such a visit for some time.

He felt sure that the recent incident that occurred on the

podium after the Cup would inspire an unwelcome visit from one or more officers of the law.

"Who's t-there?" Rocco stammered, clutching the silver toilet plunger thingy from the sausaginator and brandishing it like a weapon towards the shadows that lined the factory walls.

But there was no answer. He peered into the void. Nothing. No police officers were there to arrest him. No angry, butthurt nephew was there to berate him. No jobsworth accountant from the Lumpy Bottom tax office was there to collect.

Rocco Parmigiana could see nothing.

He waited a few more minutes before turning back to the sausaginator and plunging the STPT back down into it somewhat aggressively.

Just as he began to relax into the cathartic process of finely mincing things, Rocco felt a hand grab him by the back of the neck. This time, rather than stand up, Rocco's neck hairs thought it best to lie down immediately, and his knees turned to jellymeat.

"Wha-ha-haa-argggh," was the word that left Rocco's lips right as a meaty hand clutched him up and dangled him over the green-looking plastic dog bowl type object.

"You've just stuffed your last snag, Parmigiana," a deep, ominous voice prophesised. Rockingham Winklebutt (aka Rocco Parmigiana) heard a strange clanking and clunking coming from the Sausaginator Mark III as his life flashed before his eyes.

CHAPTER 42

ANGELITA THE BEATER

Decades ago...

Many, many years earlier, even before Google was invented, a group of students loitered around a sports oval.

"Let's go, students! Let's go! Show me some commitment. Remember, only the top five will make the senior representative team for the Cross County Knock-Outs Tournament."

Angeli (or Angelita, as she was then known) ran another lap of the oval without even puffing. At fifteen years of age, she was the favourite to make the senior representative danger ball team.

The name danger ball was confusing to those unaware of the game's history, since there was no ball of any sort used. The sport of danger ball was similar to dodgeball, except the court was smaller, there were only six players on each team, and players threw a brick at each other rather than a ball.

The name, of course, came from the game's inventor – Max McBalls, grandfather of self-help guru Ace. Originally called 'Dangerous Hardbrick McBalls', the name was shortened for brevity and due to changing social standards.

The 'danger' for which the sport was now named remained very much part of the game's appeal.

The sport was not for the scared, the weak, or those with soft skulls. Luckily, Angelita was none of those – or not the first two. In all honesty, no one had ever tested the firmness of her skull with any objective measuring tools. Several students who had been involved in fights with her could confirm that she had a thick skull that tended to collide with the noses of people she disliked. This habit of Angelita's body parts impacting with other students' faces was holding back her sporting career, but it had resulted in the menacing on-field nickname of 'Angelita the Beater'.

Angelita rather liked it. She could beat anyone, and she very often did.

"You're an exceptional athlete, Angelita," Coach Fatherington had said in a genuinely soft tone the last time Angelita had gifted a competitor a free trip in an ambulance. He'd put his hand on her shoulder. "But you must stop hospitalising the other students."

"But he started it. Did you hear what he called me? He said I was gorg—"

"I don't need to know, and it doesn't matter. Rockingham's parents have agreed to drop the charges, but you're on your last warning. If it happens again, even I won't be able to stop you from being kicked off the team."

"But it's not fair," Angelita moaned – correctly, because it wasn't fair. Then again, life isn't fair. Most things one encounters in one's lifetime are not at all fair. Only a small number of things in the world are fair, but I can't think of many, apart from the Potters Crumpy Annual Pig and Poke-a-Bear Fair, which still probably isn't at all fair from a bear's perspective.

In recent years, due to complaints from bear rights activists, it had been changed to the Potato and Poke-a-Pumpkin Fair.

It was nowhere near as successful, either for the organisers or for the professional bears, many of whom once earned a reasonable wage from the local poking fairs. In fact, almost any animal could be involved in these events, the object of which was to make the bears fall into a pit of rancid custard. Bears generally did not mind this, since the custard was usually lukewarm, which most bears felt was just right.

The role of the bears, understandably, was to pretend to be bitterly upset and offended at falling into the custard, which was all part of the show. The crowd would be emotionally invested, with the bears portraying the bad guys and the pigs playing the good guys. It was all an act, but a good bear could be very convincing, and even a mediocre pig could be persuasive with a slap of lipstick.

Bear activists argued that such events were cruel and demeaning. Bears argued that it was how they earnt a living and they needed the money to prepare for hibernation. The bear activists took the matter to the High Court and were able to ban such events in most of the Upper Colon Counties. Bears were somewhat upset about this, as it caused significant financial hardship for many and meant some had to delay or miss their winter hibernation, which made them very grumpy indeed.

The bear activists did not particularly care, since none of them were bears or needed to hibernate. By an unusual happenstance, one of the bear activists was eaten by a hangry non-hibernating bear. The others still did not particularly care. But the point is: life's not fair, and young Angelita was about to find that out.

"Angelita, Angelita. Cuz, cuzzie, bro, pass, pass! Angeli!"

Angelita looked left, where her rotund cousin was already pink in the face and screaming like a banshee. She didn't really know what a banshee was, but she was certain that if there was a banshee, her cousin Phil would be the 'banhee' version of one – although she was careful not to make any assumptions about her cousin's masculinity. Despite that, the way Phil had pulled his danger ball shorts up nearly to his armpits left little to assume.

Ignoring Phil, who couldn't throw a brick if his life depended on it – and it sometimes did in danger ball – Angelita looked right. *Damn, Rockingham!*

Rockingham was a not-quite-incompetent danger ball player. He had a good arm on him, but it was often busily involved with picking his nose or scratching his rather poky-out ears. The other arm on him was, rather unfortunately, his sinister side, which couldn't catch a cold let alone a speedily bowled brick. Plus, ever since Angeli, in a fit of inspired danger ball passion, had used Rockingham's shoulders as a platform to launch herself over the head of Kirsty Knickertwist to win last year's All Colon Counties Danger Ball Dash, breaking Rockingham's collarbone in the process, he had been making eyes at her.

His parents had threatened Angeli with a trip to juvenile hall if she so much as touched their precious golden child again.

Rockingham, however, would have very much appreciated Angelita touching him almost anywhere, except, of course, the back of his left knee, which was his secret tickle spot that made him giggle like he'd eaten a helium balloon.

Angelita frantically looked behind her for some other player, but the others were all bogged down in a complicated sort of ruck.

She was out of options.

Phil. Rockingham ... Rockingham. Phil. She looked between the two. Either of them had the potential to lose them this game, which, as well as being a representative trial, was the inaugural Potters Crumpy All Ages All Genders All Abilities Danger Ball Slam (or PCAAAGAADBS, as it was to become known), and

Angelita was no loser. She wanted that representative team spot and that trophy. The reward was a single golden-flecked brick that was shaped, appropriately, into a stylised figure of a player of no discernible age, gender or ability.

"Angeliiiiita. Come on! Cuz, cuz. Pass! Pass to meeee!" Phil was begging for her to chuck a brick at him.

Rocco just stood blushing and gaping in awe.

Angelita felt caught between a brick and a hard place. In desperation, she launched the danger brick high into the air. Just before it plummeted back to earth, Angelita shot through the lanky legs of the person she believed to be the opposing team's left lock, Quentin Snootersnout, hoping to grab the brick again herself on the other side, but she had underestimated Phil's enthusiasm. Her cousin, too, had leapt for the brick. And he, too, had failed.

That was when they all heard the loud *thunk-grunt* of a not very lithe teenage boy in Lycra™ dropping to the ground with a broken nose.

Head injuries weren't uncommon in the sport of danger ball. In any given game, at least two players went down with severe concussion and another two were usually embroiled in a retributory brawl.

But to knock a player out stone cold and break their nose with a falling brick to the face was typically frowned upon. Even worse was the sound that issued from her cousin's mouth when he finally came to his senses.

In another indication that Angelita had a very hard skull indeed, Phil woke up clutching his nether regions and squealing like a pig who'd just been poked by a very hungry bear.

From the side line, Coach Fatherington shook his head and sighed before blowing his whistle. "Below the belt," he yelled, making the universally accepted gesture for such, which was knocking his knees together, poking his tongue sideways from his mouth, crossing his eyes and moaning.

"Angelita, you've gone and done it this time. You've knocked Phil into the middle of next week, broken his hooter, and simultaneously rendered him incapable of having children," said Coach Fatherington. He held up a red card. "I'm afraid there's nothing else I can do. From now on, you're banned from danger ball, Angelita."

"But s-sir," stammered Rockingham in her defence. "Angelita the Beater is our best player. That's not fair."

"Well neither is a pig in a poke," sighed Coach Fatherington, who was referring, of course, to an antiquated idiom dated to 1855, whereby a corrupt Winklebutty farmer had sold a plump little porker sight unseen at market but had instead delivered a scrawny cat in a sack. A sack was known as a 'poke' in those days, before the common parlance of poke altered the meaning.

It was little wonder that Angelita had no idea what he meant! But nevertheless, life was, and is, unfair, and CAFEO was not wrong about that, even if they had recently banned any retelling of this sordid porcine–feline swap tale on the basis that things never ended well for cats that ended up in sacks or pokes.

"Now, run to the office to call an ambulance," Coach Fatherington instructed. And fetch an ice pack, Rocco. I'm afraid Angelita the Beater will just have to find a less bloodthirsty sport to excel at."

And she had: whippet racing.

Phil, however, had not. That incident spelled the end of Phil's danger ball career.

His parents had determined that danger ball was far too dangerous for a child with a bent hooter like his.

"Another brick to the face could drive the lad's vomer bone right up into his congenitally thick skull," the family paediatrician had insisted.

Never would that coveted, androgynous, golden-bricked statuette sit on either of their mantels.

As a result of Angelita the Beater's suspension, the school faced ongoing ridicule for having the least dangerous danger ball team in the county, driving Coach Fatherington to pack up and move away to Little Tinkle.

On the plus side, Phil's voice became two octaves higher that day, and as he was already a mezzo-soprano, he went on to sing falsetto in the Potters Crumpy Porcine, Ursine and Hystricine Children's Choir – a group renowned throughout the Lower and Middle Colon Counties, but not for their melodies.

CHAPTER 43
CHIHUAHUA SAUSAGES

"Tofu? Why would there be mushroom tofu in sausages?" said Sally-Dee.

"Maybe they're cheaper. Maybe he's trying to cut costs?"

"Mushrooms aren't cheap. And truffle mushrooms are ridiculously expensive and extremely hard to get."

"Humperdinck? Humperdinck! What in the blazes is going on down there, Mr Humperdinck!" blared a voice from the loudspeaker, and not just any voice either, but the unmistakeable voice of Rocco Parmigiana. "I can hear voices! Humperdinnnnnck!"

(If you have ever heard Rocco's voice, you'll know it's very distinctive. It sounds as you'd expect an aristocratic Donald Duck to sound if he was or *were* a walrus. English teachers argue about the use of the subjunctive mood in such situations, but walruses usually will not. If, of course, you've never heard Rocco's voice before, the metaphor is likely to go completely over your head.)

Rocco had been hiding out in the panic room in the upstairs office for at least half an hour, although it was hard to be sure exactly how long it had been, since he also had a terrible concussion.

The shadowy events of earlier that evening had inspired his sudden 'safety first' approach. Rocco had come to, cold and alone on the factory floor, with a sizeable egg on his forehead, one steel-capped boot missing, and a mangled left sock.

He also had sore ears because the sausaginator was making the most terrible *CLANK-CLANK* sounds that he soon discovered were due to his missing left boot, which was firmly wedged in the green dog-bowl shaped thing. The silver plunger type thing was nowhere to be seen, although Rocco had a vague memory of firmly wedging it *somewhere* before he'd taken a short trip to unconsciousville.

When Humperdinck didn't reply, Rocco squinted down at the factory floor again. It appeared as if a group of women had arrived, or at least two women and what looked like a whippet.

The large man-shaped shadow from earlier was nowhere to be seen. One of the women looked quite officious, snooping around as if on the hunt for something.

Thank goodness, Rocco thought. *It must be the police.*

It should be noted that the reaction people have to the police arriving is not always so favourable. It also isn't the reaction Rocco would usually have had, had he not been assaulted and knocked unconscious just over half an hour earlier. Arguably, the arrival of the police often comes with the opposite reaction, although, as earlier chapters of this book have revealed, sometimes the arrival of the police is entertaining, and sometimes the police simply aren't the police at all. This time, the latter was true. And although Rocco did not know that yet, he was about to find out.

"Hold on, Officer. I'll be right down," Rocco said. His words were followed by the *click* of the panic room unlocking.

In a moment or so, a small black door bearing a sign that read: DON'T COME IN HERE EITHER. NOT EVEN YOU,

MUM! opened, and there stood the owner of Rocco Parmigiana's voice, who was, unsurprisingly, Rocco Parmigiana. He looked surprisingly surprised when he saw the trio up close.

Sally-Dee also looked surprised.

Penelope Putz looked angry and possibly insulted, although it was unclear why.

And it was difficult to judge how Melville looked because he was keeping his cards close to his chest. He was also hoping that Penelope was not angry at him.

"What are you ... er ... doing here...? You're not the police. Who are you? Do you know my mum?" said Rocco, who was already regretting leaving the panic room. "In fact, how did you even get in?"

"How about we do the asking?" Penelope, who was definitely not a police officer, interrupted.

"Door was wide open," Sally-Dee lied, pointing.

"If you're not the police, get out of my factory right now – or else!" Rocco said, also pointing towards the wide-open door.

Melville growled a very deep cheetah growl. Even to people unfamiliar with cheetah vocalisations and body language, it sounded like the sort of growl everyone but a rhinoceros would be unwise to ignore.

He hadn't been a big fan of being ridden by Chad Cheerio and bossed around by Rocco. Melville also knew that 'thre crumbes' of that poisoned cheese could have rendered him just as short-scented as Destiny was and unable to properly appreciate the pungent aroma of rhinoceros vomit ever again. That was a crime against whippet racing, and one that Fate's Fur Art had every right to be livid about.

"Ah ... Fate's Fur Art," Rocco said in recognition. "Maybe you could stay just a little while. No need for violence."

"All right, sausage stick," Penelope muttered, grabbing Rocco by the collar and giving him terrible flashbacks to the earlier incident. "Unless you want to join your sausage brethren, you'd better talk *pronto*. Why have you been trying to bankrupt Angeli Cup?"

"Bankrupt Angeli Cup? Oh no. I would never try to hurt my beloved Angelita the Beater."

Sally-Dee blinked. "Angelita the Beater? Is that meant to be an insult?"

Rocco's cheeks reddened, and he looked away. "It was her nickname in high school, before she became famous. My name in school was Rockingham Winklebutt, before I legally changed it."

"You went to school with her?"

"Well, yes. There's only one high school in Lumpy Bottom. Phil Schiessenburger went there, too. He can vouch for me. We were all on the danger ball team together." Rocco's eyes glazed over with a fine mist of nostalgic tears. "She could beat anyone, and at any moment. Such talent. Until she broke Phil's nose and balls and got kicked off the team." Rocco sighed and swiped away a tear. "I barely got to see her after that, until she became the whippet-racing world's best jockey and got so far out of my league."

Melville knew that tone. He looked at Sally-Dee and nodded.

"All I ever wanted was to have her notice me." Rocco waved a hand around the noisy factory. "That's what all this was for – all of it. If I had wealth and fame on my side, maybe she'd ..." He blinked and shook his head sadly. "But it's all an illusion. The cost of making smallgoods has shot through the roof, and people just aren't gobbling sausages like they used to." Rocco's shoulders slumped. "Maybe it's time to hang up my sausage skins and admit I've failed."

"Fair suck of the saveloy, but if you really have such a crush on Angeli Cup, why would you sabotage the cheese?" asked Penelope suspiciously.

Rocco blinked, scratched his nose, and stared at her. "What? Sabotage what? I did no such thing. Why would I sabotage my own cheese? All I wanted was for Chad and Fate's to win the Winklebutty Cup so I could pay off my debts and help Angeli save The Last Lap. That's why Chad and I cheated with Fate's Fur Art."

"Cheats never prosper," Sally-Dee scolded, waggling a finger at him.

Rocco's shoulders slumped even further, if that was possible. "You're telling me! All the money I had left was tied up in the bet I placed on Chad and Fate's to win. And it's my own fault. Of course I backed Angelita the Beater to win, but when it turned out she couldn't race. Well ..." He looked at Sally-Dee with contrition. "I'm sorry, young lady, but no one truly believed Destiny's Poo had it in her to win with you on her back, not after that expose Ethyl Winklepimple wrote."

"Not even me." Sally-Dee sighed. "I really was a terrible whippet jockey."

Penelope patted her hand consolingly.

"I should have had faith." Rocco went on berating himself. "I should have known that Angelita never would have lost, no matter what. Now, I've lost ... I've lost everything. Angelita. My Meat Emporium. My money. And my good name."

Melville wagged his tail and then half raised it.

"Melville thinks he's telling the truth," Sally-Dee piped up. "Well, except for the bit about the good name. I don't think Rocco ever had that. At least not since he became Mr Parmigiana."

Penelope was still squinting cynically. "Well, what's this, then?" She raised her third-most popular finger and showed Rocco the gooey, sausage-meaty filling thing. "Isn't this mushroom tofu?"

Rocco glanced at Sally-Dee, then at the floor, then at Penelope, and then at Melville, and, finally, back to Sally-Dee. "Er, well ... yes. It's truffle mushroom tofu to be precise. Do you like it ...? It's my new recipe. I'm trying everything I can to stay in the game."

"Well, yes. Kind of. But where's the meat?" Penelope grabbed Rocco around the collar again with both hands and started to shake him. "What poor unfortunate animals are you putting in your sausages these days? Chihuahuas? Porcupines? Whippets?"

"Gargle. Errghh ... nore ... no ... erm. Reeeeeee ..."

"Maybe you should stop shaking him?" Sally-Dee suggested.

Penelope stopped shaking, and Rocco drew in a big breath.

"There's no meat in any of my sausages," he said, shaking his head. "I'm vegetarian. Always have been."

"No meat? But you're the Sausage Baron. And doesn't your labelling say Premium Chihuahua Sausages?" Sally-Dee asked, narrowing her eyes.

"Yes. B-because they're designed *for* chihuahuas," Rocco stammered. "And they're premium. I've been told chihuahuas love them, and they're much less snappy after eating one."

"Terrible marketing strategy." Sally-Dee shook her head.

"N-none of my sausages contain m-meat. I'm actually allergic to it. I can't stand the smell of it. It makes me vomit. That's the secret I've been keeping all this time." Rocco pointed to the sign outside his factory, which read: 'Some secrets are worth keeping.'

"So, you've been lying to your customers all this time at your so-called *Meat* Emporium?" Penelope put her hands on her hips.

"Well, you shouldn't take it too literally. It's marketing, after all. In my defence, the Lower Colon Counties Food Safety, Manufacturing, Pharmacology, Corporate Labelling, Photoshopping and Misinformation/Disinformation Committee (or the LCCFSMPCLPMDC) recently ruled that it's 100% kosher to promote vegetable milks and meat-free options as planetary, palate-saving alternatives."

Fate's Fur Art gave the kind of growl you'd imagine an obligate carnivore might give upon hearing that information.

Curiously, it was much the same noise that had issued from the mouths of the local butchers and abattoir workers following the LCCFSMPCLPMDC's announcement. They had immediately formed the Consortium of Flensers, Mincers, Eviscerаters and Un-alivers to fight the ruling and had demonstrated in the streets by simultaneously sharpening all of their knives outside the LCCFSMPCLPMSDC offices.

"He's been peddling meatfakes all this time?" Penelope looked sideways at Sally-Dee. "Do you still think he is telling the truth now?"

"One way to find out, I guess," Sally-Dee answered, gesturing to the doctor's bag.

Penelope reached into her green hessian tote bag and pulled out the triangular piece of pepperoni pizza, which she had presumably been saving for just such an occasion.

"This was meant to be my lunch tomorrow." She raised the slice of pizza up to Rocco's face.

"Pepperoni!" Rocco groaned and dutifully retaliated by vomiting, mostly into her green hessian tote.

"I guess he is telling the truth," Sally-Dee said. "So, if you did not sabotage the cheese, who did?"

Rocco looked at Penelope. Penelope looked at Sally-Dee. Sally-Dee looked at Melville. Melville was far too busy wolfing down the vomitus contents of the hessian bag to make eye contact with anyone.

CHAPTER 44

POTTERS CRUMPY PENITENTIARY FOR THE IMPENITENT

Rex peered out through the steel bars across his window to the bright neon lights of Potters Crumpy. This was the first-time he had returned to his hometown since he had run away just before the PEHOSA games. He had not spoken to his father since that day.

Rex could not really see how his current predicament could improve his relationship with his dad, but he did not completely discount the possibility.

The Potter's Crumpy Penitentiary for the Impenitent overlooked the city. It had initially been built as a seafood processing plant at the height of the popularity of local seafood donuts.

Once the donut craze subsided, the factory was abandoned until it was repurposed as a prison. Its design made the conversion relatively easy.

In many ways, it was a very modern facility for its time, and inmates from the prison had the lowest re-offending rates of any gaol in the county. This was often attributed to the excellent rehabilitation provided, but it probably had more to do with the awful seafood smell that always seemed to permeate the cells.

In order to cut costs, the builders had poured the concrete

foundations of the prison over a few tons of leftover prawns, fish and squid. The result was a God-awful stench of rancid seafood.

Any person forced to spend even a brief period breathing in the foetid air vowed to change his or her or their life and never ever, *ever*, go back to that hellhole.

Rex had only just arrived and was still too distraught about his incarceration to focus too much on the smell. He reached for a cup of mouldy water and leaned back into his bunk bed.

"So, what didn't you do?" came a voice from the bed above. A small head slid across the edge of the upper bunk bed and revealed itself to Rex.

It was an unusual-looking head, even as heads go.

Heads, and more specifically human heads, are by definition strange and poorly designed. Placing the nose, which is prone to mucous discharges, above the mouth, which is most often used for eating, seems a particularly distasteful design flaw. While it is true that this makes picking and eating boogers very convenient, most would argue this is not an advantage.

Placing the ears on the side of the head, rather than the more traditional top of the head, is also very poor placement. A good whack to the ears usually results in an unpleasant head knock, rather than the more glancing blow that might occur if you were smacking ears placed atop the head.

To Rex, human noses were also unnecessarily short and lacked the moist, darkened colour of most animal noses.

This particular face was not stranger than any other human face, but it was definitely less attractive owing to the left-leaning slant of the nose, the retracted chin, and the slightly bucked teeth. With the exception of gerbils, most other inhabitants of the boroughs would agree that it was not the sort of face one would wish to attach to the body of someone they desired to take on a date or introduce to their family.

The unattractive head stretched further over the top bunk bed to reveal that it was attached to a neck and two shoulders.

"Me name is Albertonio Gorgonzola. You might have heard of me. In my prime, I was a fromager, stanky toe health campaigner and owner of the greatest cheese emporium in history – Albertonio's Cheese Bazaar."

The unattractive head's right arm stretched down to Rex and shook his paw.

Albertonio flung his legs over the side of the bed and jumped down from the top bunk. "Rex Spikington, is it? I think I read about you in the paper. The 'Trubulsom Porquapine of Potters Crumpy' they call you. Appears you sabotaged the ceremonial cheese."

Rex hung his head even lower than it already was and shook it.

"Oh, I believe you. I know a thing or two about cheese. I was a big cheese myself for a while, you might say, until that dirty dog stabbed me in the back."

Rex was not impressed by the dog metaphor. Some of his best friends were dogs. But, by all accounts, Rocco Parmigiana was a very dirty person indeed. Rex's spines quivered at the thought of him taking over The Last Lap.

"Sorry, did not mean to offend. You see, I trusted him. Thought he would be my partner and help me win the cheese wars. Turns out, he was a two-timing dirty—" *KABANG!*

The *kabang*, of course, was not Albertonio talking. It was the sound of the southern wall of the penitentiary succumbing to the stress of a large sausage truck driving smack-bang into it.

CHAPTER 45
THE LIT PRISON PARTY

It was not the first time a huge truck had driven at high speed into the outer walls of Potters Crumpy Penitentiary for the Impenitent. In fact, it was not even the thirty-first time it had happened in the long and inglorious history of the institution.

On one occasion, which the Winklebutty Bigbooty Museum and Burlesque Cabaret Restaurant's *Big Book of Prison Records* documented as the twenty-fifth time, a lorry full of vodka, mattresses, marshmallows, firecrackers and flamethrowers had somehow crashed into the gaol on bonfire night, after the driver suffered an undisclosed medical incident.

Everyone now remembered 5 November 1932 as the Lit Prison Party, when the impenitent had enjoyed a very merry evening of setting fire to just about anything they could find.

Strangely, the guards had not enjoyed the bonfire as much. Most of them still refused to commemorate the occasion.

Each year, prisoners remember it by holding up two fingers in an inverted V for Victory (or some say *V for Vendetta*) sign, which became a popular hand gesture to signify to the guards that, despite the fireworks chicanery, the bravest of prisoners still had their most-popular fingers.

In the gaol's most recent Anonymous Impenitent Incarceration Survey, it was voted the penitentiary's second-most popular hand gesture. The first most-popular gesture was the one made to signify a below the belt hit, which was also the one used to attract the attention of prison medics.

Half an hour before this particular sausage truck hurtled through the walls of the penitentiary, damaging the façade and severing at least one sewage pipeline before crashing into the cell Albertonio Gorgonzola and the now widely reviled Cheese Poisoning 'Trubulsom Porquapine' of Lumpy Bottom (aka Rex Spikington Junior) shared, Penelope Putz had been holding up her least-popular fingers to reveal Rocco Parmigiana's meatfake ruse.

Just as Fate's Fur Art had finished devouring his vomitus delicacy, and right as Rocco Parmigiana was beginning to regain some of his colour, Rocco's security detail had arrived.

"Well, about time, Humperdinck," Rocco Parmigiana had groaned, still bent over double.

"Who're all these then, Boss?" Mr Humperdinck said. "Don't look real scary to me, does they?" Humperdinck squinted at Sally-Dee and fingered his gappy teeth with his tongue (if a tongue could finger anything, which is already rather a messy analogy, so let's forget about that and just state that Mr Humperdinck's tongue was busily engaged in trying to prise out a large chunk of his evening meal that was wedged between his upper right canine and incisor).

"Well, er, no. I guess not," Rocco answered. "But you're also Head of Warehouse Security, and we've had some ... er ... security breaches."

"Speaking of heads, what's that on yours?" Penelope asked,

jerking her chin towards the large, swollen nodule on Rocco's forehead. "It looks like it needs medical attention."

Rocco rubbed the lump. "Ah, just a ... ah, a not-so-little 'incident' I need to talk to my Head of Security about later." He frowned at Mr Humperdinck.

Penelope pulled a flashlight from her bag, wiped residual traces of vomit off it, and shone it directly into Rocco's eyes.

"Gah," said Rocco, immediately throwing up his hands to block the bright light.

"Just as I thought," Penelope said triumphantly. "Mr Parmigiana, you've just been diagnosed with a bad case of concussion. You'd best come with me right away."

"Listen here, I don't know who you think you are, but you're not a police officer, so you can't just waltz in here unannounced and force me to come with you."

"Firstly, we didn't 'waltz' in here," Penelope Putz interrupted with a sniff. "Just because we're women you think we waltz everywhere? No, sir. We scaled the walls." She pulled the grappling hook from her bag and menaced him with it. "And secondly" – she turned to Mr Humperdinck – "we ARE scary. Why would you say we're not scary? Is it because we're girls? Are you saying the sisterhood isn't scary? We may not be scarier than bears, mister, but we're still terrifying once you get to know us." She jabbed her most popular pointer finger right in his face.

Melville padded towards Humperdinck and growled scarily for good measure.

"Er, sorry," Mr Humperdinck replied humbly, looking between his boss and the strange woman whose fingers were all doing obnoxious things. "I don' think me work cover pays out for this sorta thing, Boss." He took a step back.

"Humperdinck, you colossal nincompoop. You don't have any work cover. And you've been extremely lax with security. What if the machines *had* been mincing? They could have sued me."

Rocco berated him. "What if they'd been from the tax office? Or from the Consortium of Flensers, Mincers, Eviscerators and Un-alivers? You know how much they hate me." Rocco was shaking with anger and adrenaline. "What if it had been that awful man – whatever his name was – Bernie, Vernie, Bork from the bank? You know they've been sniffing around ever since we lost that bet."

"Sorry, Boss," Humperdinck said, ducking his head.

"Well, we may be girls, but we don't have time for all this chit-chat," Penelope spoke up. "If Rocco isn't responsible for poisoning Chad Cheerio, we need to find out who is so we can free Rex from prison *pronto*."

Sally-Dee thought for a moment, and then a strange look came over her face. "The man from the bank," she muttered, as she pulled out her mobile phone and dialled a number. "Angeli, meet us at Potters Crumpy Penitentiary for the Impenitent in thirty minutes. Rocco did not sabotage the cheese, but I think I know who did."

"I agree. Rocco did sabotage the cheese," Angeli Cup replied. "He should be in gaol!"

At that stage, Sally-Dee remembered Angeli Cup's bizarre selective hearing loss. "Trust me, just come to the gaol. I'll explain when we get there."

CHAPTER 46
IT WAS THEM THAT DONE IT

"I wish you'd told us to wait *outside* the gaol." Angeli Cup coughed as she wiped off her blue jodhpurs and patted down Destiny's fur.

The enormous sausage truck was lodged half-in and half-out of Rex and Albertonio's cell, with the two prisoners crouched on either side of their now crumpled bunk bed.

"Well, the plan did change somewhat after the brakes failed," Sally-Dee yelled as she clambered out of the cab. She had to yell to be heard over the noise of the still whirring and smoking engine.

"What a sturdy old girl," Rocco added, tumbling out after her. "Look at her. She's barely taken a dint in all these years."

"I'll have you mind your mouth and not talk about me like that if you please, Rocco," Angeli Cup snarled at him.

"Oh, Angelita. *My* Angelita." Rocco swept forward and caught her up in a bear hug – or it would have been one, if he was allowed to call it that, but the Bears Union of Moderation had put an end to the term.

"I wasn't talking about you. I was talking about her." Rocco pointed to the truck. "Although, you're also even tougher, stronger and more beautiful than you've ever been, Angelita." He swooned.

Rocco's sudden bravery was probably a result of his concussion. The force of the truck careening through the walls had planted his face hard into the dashboard, doubling his egghead in size.

"Good heavens! What's that knob on your noggin?" Angeli said, giving him a withering look as she wriggled free of his grasp. "You mean it wasn't the plan to drive the truck straight into Rex's cell, free him, and insert you here in his rightful place in prison?" She continued. "And what on Earth is Dr Putz doing here?"

"No. That wasn't the plan. Because Rocco is innocent," Sally-Dee elaborated. "Just like Rex is."

Rex quivered all of his quills in agreement.

"And Dr Putz is here because ... well, because..." Sally-Dee blushed a little and tidied her hair, which was white with dust from all the broken brick.

"It's complicated," Penelope interrupted. "Just like this case. But we do know that it wasn't Rocco who cut the cheese with lava peppers."

"It was them that done it," came a strange voice from the other side of the ruined bunk bed. A long, white, shaking finger appeared from the darkness and pointed in the direction of one of the people in the room.

"Yes," Sally-Dee said, following the finger's direction to the tall, lumbering figure of Mr Humperdinck, who was hunched over in the driver's seat of the vehicle. "He crashed it. He was the only one with a truck license."

"No, no. Not that," said the voice as a pale and not very attractive head followed the voice into view. "It was them that done it," Albertonio Gorgonzola said over the noise of the engine spluttering and the beep of the truck being put into reverse and revving at high speed out of the hole in the wall.

"It was that dog-eating son of a lemming Humperdinck what done it all along."

CHAPTER 47
TAKE IT TO THE BANK

Phil Schiessenburger sat tall behind a large mahogany desk and scrawled in an expensive-looking leather-bound diary. I cannot tell you exactly how much either cost him, but unless they were presents gifted to him by very satisfied clients, it was probably a whole lot – perhaps even a sum only a banker could afford.

A bulky security guard marched into the office and approached the desk. "Sir, some people to see you, Sir."

Phil gestured with his right hand without looking up. "Bring them in."

Destiny, Angeli Cup, Penelope, Sally-Dee, Fate's Fur Art and Rocco strode into the room in single file.

"Cousin! Lovely to see you." Phil smiled with the right side of his face while his left side stayed perfectly still.

"It was you, you swine! It was you all along. *You* put the lava pepper in Destiny's cheese, and you poisoned Chad's cheese, too," Angeli accused him.

Phil continued to write in his leather-bound book. "Why would I want to poison your whippet? I would have nothing to gain from hurting Destiny. Besides, I like dogs."

Angeli Cup put her hands on her hips and looked at Sally-Dee. "He's got a point, you know," she conceded.

"Because you weren't trying to poison Destiny." Penelope had a gleam in her eye. "You were trying to poison Angeli Cup."

"Why would I want my dearest cousin to lose her sense of smell?" Phil shrugged.

"You know as well as we all now do that Lumpy Bottom lava peppers are *deadly* to humans!" insisted Sally-Dee.

"It should be noted that while a Lumpy Bottom lava pepper will burn a whippet's smell receptors right out, whippets are hardy animals that nearly always survive lava pepper poisoning. Humans are less resilient.

A single lava pepper can cause irreparable brain damage, literally explosive diarrhoea, and usually death," spoke up Penelope, lapsing into doctor mode.

"But why kill my only cousin? I'm her sole living relative." Phil Schiessenburger widened his eyes innocently, adjusted his tie, and cleared his throat.

Sally-Dee narrowed her eyes again. "Because *as* her only living relative, if she died you would inherit everything she owns, including The Last Lap!"

Phil clapped his hands in an insultingly slow, deliberate fashion. "Bravo, Bravo. How clever you are. And yes, you are right. Mostly. I have had my eyes on The Last Lap for years. Could never find a way to get my hands on it. And then you, my dear small-brained cousin, won it in a game of Scrabble®. Ironic, don't you think? I gave you The Last Lap, and now I'm taking it back."

"You didn't give it to her. Angelita the Beater earned it! She won it fair and square." Rocco came to her rescue.

"Oh, come on, you didn't think 'bumfat' was a real word, did you Angeli? I made that up, along with all the other help I gave you with triple letter scores during that game. I needed you to win. I needed The Last Lap to be yours. Then, all I had to do was kill you or wait for you to go broke, and the farm would be all mine." He rubbed his hands together gleefully. "It would be fitting payment for what you did to me, *cousin* – breaking my nose, breaking my ... well other bits, and leading me to join that Godawful choir and be bullied by everyone in the entire county.

"No, I never forgot, and I most definitely never forgave. And it all would have worked perfectly – if you hadn't climbed on your moral high horse and given that stupid mutt the first bite of the cheese the first time I tried it, or if Destiny had taken the PEM this time, or if Rex hadn't gotten you disqualified and you'd both eaten that lava pepper poisoned cheese."

"But why would you want my dogs and my porcupines?" Angeli Cup put her hands on her hips.

"I don't think it was the animals he wanted,' Rocco concluded. "It was the truffle fungi, wasn't it, Schiessenburger? The ones that grow everywhere on Angeli's farm."

"You mean the mushrooms? The black mushies I feed the whippets?" Angeli's forehead furrowed in surprise. "The ones that smell like spicy meat?"

"Yes those, you utter imbecile." Phil shook his head. "After the fungi eradication campaign, those truffles became so rare that their price shot through the roof. Almost no areas were unaffected – except your farm. Its location made it inaccessible to the aerial spraying. It is pristine, completely unaffected by the poison. Those truffles are now worth upwards of a thousand shillings a punnet, and I have a very willing buyer in your boyfriend Rocco's moronic henchman, Mr Humperdinck, who does all the actual work of making the Lumpy Bottom Meat Emporium's sausages. We might as well own it. And when we do, those black truffles will make us a fortune.

"And there you were, cousin, feeding them to your idiotic dogs and porcupines for five years. But finally – *finally!* –they're mine," Phil said in a classic villain-divulges-all type monologue. He stood up from his desk, and his large, man-shaped shadow spread over them along with his creepy Disney-villain laugh, which is not the sort of sound I can imitate without appearing stupid, but it sounded something like, "Haa, harrgh, ha, hargh, ho haahah hargh harrgggggh!"

"It was YOU," Rocco gasped. "*You* were the man-sized shadow who tried to toss me in the Sausaginator!"

"And I would have succeeded, too," boasted Schiessenburger, "if it wasn't for these two nosey nobodies and their blinged-up greyhound sniffing around right at the worst possible time." Phil waved a meaty arm at Penelope, Sally-Dee, and Fate's Fur Art. "I asked Humperdinck to do it, but he insisted he didn't want to mess up the machine with human meat. He kept rabbiting on about 'Making Sausages Great Again' and 'Putting meat back on the menu, boys', and muttering something about whippet body fat and velvet margarine.

"To be honest, I didn't understand what Humperdinck was talking about half the time, but he seemed very keen to start clearing out The Last Lap. Where is Humperdinck anyway?" Phil looked directly at Rocco.

"He took off. Stole my sausage truck and he's gone on the run. I've already put in a police report with Constable Oregano."

"Even better. Now the entire enterprise will be all mine!" Phil laughed again and reached into his drawer, pulling out a small black wooden box about the size of an average small wooden box. He lifted the lid. "See these little beauties." He grabbed a truffle and swallowed it whole. "Pure gold. Hundreds of shillings each. And now, all the truffles are mine." He grabbed a second and swallowed it whole, too. "Thank you, dear cousin. And, might I add, there is absolutely nothing you can do about it. I've done nothing illegal."

"You nearly killed Chad, you destroyed Destiny's smell,

you've had Rex unjustly locked up, and you tried to mince Rocco in a Sausaginator. I think the police might be interested in that, don't you?" Penelope listed his crimes on her busy fingers.

"Well, yes. Some of that would be considered below the belt." Phil made the universal gesture for below the belt, which had been a bit of a sore point ever since Angeli had ended his chance of fathering children.

"Still, it's rather a handy alibi I have, don't you think, being that I'm the head of the Whippet Racing Tribunal." Phil waggled his bushy eyebrows. Then he grabbed a third truffle and swallowed it whole, too. "You, my dear cousin, might be joining Humperdinck in prison, since you are his business partner and obvious accomplice." He pushed the leather-bound diary across the table for Sally-Dee to read.

"This says you took money from Humperdinck. Why would you do that, Angeli?" Sally turned towards her.

"That's a lie." Angeli objected, setting her hands on her hips.

"Well, yes it is. But it matters not." Phil smirked as he downed another truffle. "That cheque I wrote for you was a direct transfer from Humperdinck's personal account. A little insurance policy in case I ever needed to link you to him. I think Constable Oregano will be extremely interested in you being in cahoots with Mr Humperdinck. You, my dear cousin, have been, well and truly framed."

Angeli bit her bottom lip. She was trying to think of a witty retort, but she couldn't.

"Now, if you don't mind," Phil sneered. "I am a bit busy. My security guards will happily show you all the door." He jerked his chin towards his goons.

Sally-Dee was astute enough to notice that neither guard was smiling, nor did either of them appear especially loyal. They both appeared very big and possibly very angry. Just as she was about to raise this issue with Phil, he spoke before she could. "Would you mind escorting my … my…" Phil coughed and swallowed uncomfortably. His skin reddened and sweat beaded his forehead.

A soft squealing sound issued to his left. Phil turned, and there, standing on his hind legs behind Phil's desk was Rex, who had snuck in completely unnoticed behind Destiny.

"R-Rex," Sally-Dee stammered. She knew the look on the porcupine's face meant he was up to mischief. "You haven't done what I think you've done, have you?"

Rex lifted two of his right lower quills and smiled. A growing rumbling sound came from Phil's tummy. His face turned purple, and his belt expanded.

"RUN FOR IT! He's going to blow!" Penelope yelled.

Angeli, Rocco, Sally-Dee, Penelope, Destiny and Rex all sprinted past the exit sign and out the front door of the bank.

"How many Lumpy Bottom lava peppers did you put in those truffles?" Sally-Dee asked, puffing.

Rex wiggled two of his back spines.

"What did he say?" Penelope puffed.

"All of them. Run faster!"

They made it out of the front entrance of the bank, down the main road and to the corner of Ramsbottom and Snorthoggle before they felt the radiant heat of the explosion. The sonic boom hit seconds later, throwing them across the intersection. The smell of burnt toilet water followed immediately.

Destiny was the first to rise. She was shaken, but otherwise okay. Luckily, she could not smell a thing. Sally-Dee came next. She could smell very well and immediately wished she couldn't. One by one, the rest of them climbed to their feet.

Penelope looked back to where, two seconds before, the Last National Winklebutty Bank had stood. The dust was already settling over the rubble. The golden dome was gone. The plinths and pillars had all collapsed. The front facade still stood, but the letters had totally fallen off. Penelope shrugged. "I guess it really was the *Last* National Winklebutty Bank after all."

The din of overlapping police and ambulance sirens filled the air.

"Well, well, well, what have we here?" announced Constable Oregano.

CHAPTER 48

SAUSAGE-EATING MAGGOTS

"Will he pull through, Dr Putz?" Sally-Dee raised her eyebrows and appeared to almost be upset.

"Can't really be sure." Penelope Putz shrugged.

"Well, I'm sure he is in good hands. If not, I hear Ernie is pretty fast with that trolley down to G floor." Sally-Dee twirled her hair with her right hand while Rex tried to overcome his urge to vomit at the blatant flirting.

Sergeant Pavlova and Constable Oregano approached through the doorway. "Well, we'd better give Mr Schiessenburger some privacy for his R & R." Dr Putz smiled at Sally-Dee. "Care to join me for a coffee?"

"When will we be able to interrogate Mr Schiessenburger," Constable Oregano asked in a tone that was soft like battery acid.

"Hard to say. He has fifth-degree burns to his throat and backside. Worst case I've ever seen."

"I thought Lumpy Bottom lava pepper only burnt the rear end?"

"Usually, but this was an ultra-high-pressure explosion. It came out both ends. I've never seen that before. The patient lost both bum cheeks, left face cheek, and half his tongue. He is very unlucky to be alive."

"You mean *lucky* to be alive, don't you?"

"No, I really don't."

"Er ... is it painful?"

"Well, let's just say it's like a colony of gerb—"

"Let's not bore them with medical details, Dr Putz," Sally-Dee interrupted. "What happened to Albertonio?"

"We've released him," Constable Oregano replied. "Turns out he had nothing to do with sabotaging the cheese and it was his assistant ..." She looked at her notepad. "One *Mr Humperdinck*, who had blown up his cheese factory all those years ago. Something about a dispute over Humperdinck spiking the smallgoods with dog meat.

"Then there was that 'thing' about the stinky toe cheese public health campaign, but everyone seems to have forgotten about that, so Gorgonzola has been entirely pardoned." Constable Oregano lowered her voice to a not-quite-whisper. "He's probably back on his private island off Weinercrump. But don't worry, apparently he still owes a ton of taxes. Sooner or later, I'll find something to pin on that little sausage-eating maggot again, and I'll put him away for a very, very long time."

Constable Pavlova whispered to Olivia Oregano, who sighed audibly. "Apparently, I'm not supposed to call him a little sausage-eating maggot," she said. "PC culture is destroying good police work."

CHAPTER 49

12 RULES FOR SPINES: AN ANTIDOTE TO PEACE

Close to a year later

It was 29 September, and the 114th Winklebutty Cup was just two days away.

"Don't you wish you were racing, Destiny? You're still a chance to be the first six-and-a-half-time winner," Penelope teased.

Destiny lay on the brand-new luxurious leather couch, her tummy extending over the pillows. Rex waddled over and gently placed his paw on her belly.

"Not long to go now, Destiny." Angeli Cup looked over at Sally-Dee and smiled. "I hope it's a girl."

Penelope's eyes narrowed, and her lips puckered. "Or a boy. Or whatever. As long as it is a healthy and super-fast porcupet or whippupine, or whatever."

After the last Winklebutty Cup, a number of very serious meetings of the Whippet Racing Tribunal were held. Victory was eventually awarded to both Destiny's Poo and Foot Fungus

Fromage. Since it was a joint win, Destiny was awarded a half a victory, making her the only five-and-a-half-time victor.

Fate's Fur Art was disqualified. But Melville didn't mind. He joined the newly refurbished The Last Lap as a personal trainer and pilates instructor. When he wasn't working, he would go to The Fox and Whippet on open mic nights and follow his dream of becoming the first cheetah stand-up comedian.

Angeli Cup used the winnings to pay off the bank and refurbish The Last Lap with Sally-Dee's help. They now run a successful black truffle fungi wholesale business, which covers the retirement home's running costs. Rocco Parmigiana gets free truffles and has continued to expand his vegan sausage empire with Angeli's help, since the two are now dating. They are taking things one day at a time.

Destiny and Rex were married in an intimate ceremony in Potters Crumpy, which was only the second time Rex had been back there since he first ran away from home. This time, he was not in handcuffs.

Rex's parents attended, and based on their reactions, both were very proud. Destiny is expected to give birth at any time.

Sally-Dee and Penelope Putz are also engaged, although they haven't yet set a date. Penelope is sick of people asking when they're getting married, so I would strongly advise against that line of conversation.

Phil Schiessenburger eventually recovered from his injuries and was discharged from hospital ten months after he was admitted. In a medical first, he became the only person to receive a double butt cheek implant. Unfortunately, the left implant exploded a week later, resulting in him being readmitted to hospital. Chad Cheerio was also discharged and, against all odds, went on to ride again.

The whereabouts of one Mr Nigel Humperdinck remain unknown. Ethyl Winklepimple's 'WHAT'S UP WINKLEBUTTY?' broke the news that a police search of his living quarters revealed Humperdinck was a secret member of the Consortium for Flensers, Mincers, Evisceraters and Un-alivers. The *Lumpy Bottom Examiner* later serialised the poorly spelt manifesto Humperdinck had written outlining his plan to 'Make Sausages Meaty Again' by eviscerating and mincing the entire list of residents of The Last Lap one by one, starting with Bugsby Pratwaffle, who had apparently once tattooed something unsavoury on Humperdinck's back.

As for me, Ace McBalls, I eventually finished my legal studies and became a qualified lawyer, which should come in handy because I've got a feeling this won't be the last time we hear of Phil Schiessenburger or Nigel Humperdinck.

My documentary expose on the 113th Winklebutty Cup, titled *How a Banker's Butt Went Bang* won *Whippet Racing Monthly*'s 'Pupperazzi' award for journalistic excellence.

Currently, I'm working on two new best-selling self-help books by Ace McBalls: *How to Win Without Getting Caught Cheating* and a confidence guide for porcupines titled *12 Rules for Spines: An Antidote to Peace.*

THE END

About the So-Called Author

Ace McBalls is the pseudonym of Australian author Riccardo N Caniato. When he is not writing books, he spends his time minding his own business – and he recommends you do the same.

ABSOLUTELY 100% REAL REVIEWS

"One of the best books I've ever written, by a long way."
—Ace K McBalls

"It's okay, I guess. There's a bit of bad language, which I don't like. It could have been a bit shorter."
—Mavis McBalls

"That's how long books are meant to be, Mum! And you need saucy language to keep the audience engaged."
—Ace K McBalls

"A fart-a-minute romp that made me howl with derision."
—Ethyl Winklepimple

"Won off the wurst things I evah fur-kin red."
—Bugsby Pratwaffle

"I couldn't be bothered reading it, but Destiny says it's okay."
—Nathaniel Spikington Jnr

"Most of you won't even know you've got it until you get it."
—Albertonio Gorgonzola

The cheesiest thing since the 103rd Winklebutty Cup ceremony."
—Earl Autumnrump

"Kept me in stitches!"
—Dr Penelope Putz

"A galloping satire guaranteed to give you the trots.* "
— The Editor

*Guarantees not guaranteed, warrantied, warranted, mandated or parodied.

The publisher wholly indemnifies itself against all and any harms, perceived harms, insults, inferred insults, microaggressions, macroaggressions, transgressions, assaults, butthurts, arsehats, slurs implied or intended, swears, blasphemies, jokes, bad jokes, dad jokes, bear fights, cat fights, pigs in blankets or lipstick, pillow fights, prison breaks and digestive upsets, as well as any other complaints, warranted or unwarranted, written, spoken, sung, conveyed by interpretive dance, virtue-signalled, hand-gestured, or carried over a carriage service before or after midnight.

No lemmings, beavers or chihuahuas were harmed during the making of this book.

www.ingramcontent.com/pod-product-compliance
Lightning Source LLC
Chambersburg PA
CBHW010318100726
47906CB00006B/1048

* 9 7 8 0 9 9 4 2 3 1 0 1 7 *